Also by Beth Turley

If This Were a Story
The Last Tree Town

Beth Turley

Simon & Schuster Books for Young Readers

New York   London   Toronto   Sydney   New Delhi

For all best friends, especially mine

SIMON & SCHUSTER BOOKS FOR YOUNG READERS
An imprint of Simon & Schuster Children's Publishing Division
1230 Avenue of the Americas, New York, New York 10020

SIMON & SCHUSTER BOOKS FOR YOUNG READERS
and related marks are trademarks of Simon & Schuster, Inc.
For information about special discounts for bulk purchases, please contact
Simon & Schuster Special Sales at 1-866-506-1949 or business@simonandschuster.com.
The Simon & Schuster Speakers Bureau can bring authors to your live event.
For more information or to book an event, contact the Simon & Schuster Speakers Bureau
at 1-866-248-3049 or visit our website at www.simonspeakers.com.
Interior design by Tom Daly
The text for this book was set in Adobe Caslon Pro.
Manufactured in the United States of America
0721 FFG
First Edition
2 4 6 8 10 9 7 5 3 1
Library of Congress Cataloging-in-Publication Data
Names: Turley, Beth, author.
Title: The Flyers / Beth Turley.
Description: First edition. | New York : Simon & Schuster Books for Young Readers, [2021] | Audience:
Ages 8–12. | Audience: Grades 4–6. |
Summary: Picked to become an intern at her favorite teen magazine and spend an adventure-packed summer, between seventh and eighth grades, in New York City, Elena is excited but also worried about losing her best friend.
Identifiers: LCCN 2020050952 (print) | LCCN 2020050953 (ebook) |
ISBN 9781534476721 (hardcover) | ISBN 9781534476745 (ebook)
Subjects: CYAC: Best friends—Fiction. | Friendship—Fiction. | Internship programs—Fiction. |
Periodicals—Publishing—Fiction. | New York (N.Y.)—Fiction.
Classification: LCC PZ7.1.T875 Fl 2021 (print) | LCC PZ7.1.T875 (ebook) |
DDC [Fic]—dc23
LC record available at https://lccn.loc.gov/2020050952
LC ebook record available at https://lccn.loc.gov/2020050953

Acknowledgments

My sister and I used to read magazines together obsessively. Delivery days were the best days, and we had our rituals for all the different sections. I am so thankful to my editor, Krista Vitola, and the entire team at S&S Books for Young Readers for allowing me to write the magazine book of my dreams, and to Celia Krampien for a beautiful cover to match. I am also lucky to have Zoe Sandler, who saw the *Bold Type* potential in these characters, as my agent.

Thank you to my parents for their guidance and for the many subscriptions to *Discovery Girls*, *Highlights*, and *Seventeen*. I learned so much from those magazines, and from you both. Thank you to my sister, Cristina, for honoring our traditions. To every member of my big, funny family—I have felt support and excitement from all of you. Thank you for your jokes and love. And to my writing family at Western Connecticut State University: nothing is better than when we're all together.

I dedicated this book to all best friends, especially mine, because I could not ask to have more generous, bold, and brilliant people to call my friends. You are all my Flyers.

Interested in writing?
Fashion?
Photography?

 ·

Are you a Spread Your Wings *magazine superfan?*
Apply now to be a Flyer! Selected Flyers get to spend five days in
New York City, and are a critical part of the development of the
September issue. This program helps budding journalists see just
what it takes to work at our iconic magazine through hands-
on experience, writing workshops, staff meetings, and best of all,
New York City adventures.

To apply, you must submit (1) up to five photos that
represent you, (2) your personal questionnaire and contact
information sheet, and (3) a writing sample.

Unfortunately, we can only select four Flyers for the
program, so if your application is not accepted, we urge you
to try again next year.

Good luck!

Fly High,
The Spread Your Wings *Internship Team*

· ·

Chapter One

—

The Text

Summer and I read *Spread Your Wings* magazine the way some people read mystery novels—in one big, exhilarating gulp. Summer's favorite part was the essays at the end, written by other *Spread Your Wings* readers like us. In the September issue, it was the four chosen Flyers who wrote them. My favorite was the Ask Amelia advice column. It was like always receiving the right diagnosis and treatment to life's problems. *Crush doesn't like you back? Diagnosis: broken heart. Treatment: remember how great you are anyway. (And if that doesn't work, throw eggs at said crush's house.)*

I imagined writing *egg house* into the yellow notepad I'd have when I grew up and became a therapist, mending broken hearts.

"This Flyer was on the US national swimming team.

How do we compete with that, Elena?" Summer asked. Her words rushed out like a fast-moving train. Hyper-speed was her default setting.

She twirled a red chunk of hair tight around her finger. We sat on my bed with a bag of Bugles and last year's September issue of *Spread Your Wings* in front of us. Even though we both had our own subscriptions, we still liked to flip through one copy together. Summer kept hers safe in a plastic bin underneath her bed.

"You done?" Summer would ask when we read.

"Almost," I'd say.

Summer read fast. I liked to do things carefully, absorb each word and let it sit in my brain until I was certain I understood what it meant.

"We compete by being number one fans." I pointed across the room. I didn't keep my issues in a bin; Summer and I cut them up and taped them to my baby blue wall. Pages from the past two years of *Spread Your Wings* covered every inch of space, pictures and articles and Letters from the Editor, Akshita Balay. Bright pink (Summer's) and yellow (mine) Post-it notes glowed in between the pages with our thoughts written on them. Practice for if we were ever picked to be Flyers and got to write our own essays for the magazine.

"Yeah, but." Summer inhaled a Bugle. "Only one of us should use it, we can't have our applications looking the same." Crumbs fell from her mouth and onto the comforter.

She brushed them away with the back of her hand. Best friends aren't grossed out by things like that, especially best friends since birth. Especially best friends who live right next door to each other. Our parents liked to tell the story of the first time we met, in our strollers, at the spot where our yards connect. They say we looked at each other like we knew we were being introduced to someone important.

We both stared down at the pages for a second. The paper was so glossy I could see the silhouettes of our heads almost touching.

"You can use the wall," I said to the recipe for banana cream pudding.

She lifted her head and I could feel her looking at me.

"No, I couldn't, it's your wall, you should use it."

"I want you to," I said, eyes glued to the recipe.

When I snuck a glance at her she was smiling, her left dimple peeking out. I called it her Truly Happy Dimple. It warmed me up like *actual* summer. Like sunshine and salty air. The light at the end of a dark winter. I would've done anything to make Summer smile. Teachers told her to slow down when she talked. And when she took tests. And when she burst down the hallway like a red-haired hurricane. But I liked being the only one who could keep up with her. I was her personal storm watcher.

Even if that storm had been hitting a little harder lately.

"Thanks, Elena, you don't need to use the wall to get

chosen anyway, you're great enough without it." The sentence was a gushy blur.

"Yeah, right." I studied the recipe. *Three bananas, 1 cup of sugar, 1 tsp. of vanilla.* If there was a recipe for me, Elena Martinez, it would be three tablespoons of dreams of becoming a therapist, five ounces of family, and one million cups of socially awkward. Summer was the only person I could talk to without my face blushing cherry red. Her recipe would include one pair of running shoes, ten bags of red Skittles, and unlimited scoops of the stars above our houses when we talked from our windows at night.

Summer looked over, and her long ponytail skimmed the pages.

"Don't say that," she said. "You are the fabulous Elena. The best student in our whole class. The most perfect penmanship I've ever seen. *And* my best friend."

I leaned my shoulder into hers. I knew she'd understand it meant *thank you.* The next page of the magazine was the "Have Your Best First Day of School Ever" article, which was funny because we were only a month away from the *last* day of seventh grade. Instead of rereading *Spread Your Wings's* tips on locker organization and cute lunchboxes, I thought about how in one month it would be vacation, full of long, school-less days with Summer. No different schedules keeping us apart, no classmates driving wedges between us.

"You done?" she asked a few minutes later.

"Almost," I said.

A buzzing sound came from Summer's bag on the floor. She rolled off the bed and landed on the carpet with a *thud.*

"Are you okay?" I asked. I leaned my head over. Summer was sprawled on the ground, reading a text.

"Yup," she said. The Truly Happy Dimple reappeared in her cheek.

Summer stood up from the carpet, hair in her eyes. She picked up her backpack and started throwing her things inside. The half-finished bag of Bugles, her sunglasses, the *Spread Your Wings* we were reading.

"What are you doing?" I asked.

"Didn't I tell you? I have plans with Riah."

"Santangelo?"

"Yeah."

Riah was in my language arts class, and was on the cross-country team with Summer, but she wasn't someone Summer had ever rushed out of my room to hang out with before.

"No, you didn't tell me," I said. "I thought we were going to work on our applications."

"I'll do some of it at home and then we can finish another day." She swung her backpack over her shoulder.

"But you need a picture of the wall," I said, hoping I didn't sound whiny about her leaving.

"I'll take one later, Elena."

She seemed annoyed and her smile was fading. It pricked

me like a sharp pin. I could tell I was latching on to Summer too hard, like a tick, like something she couldn't get rid of. She pushed her feet into her running shoes. My name was scrawled in purple marker on the toes. Summer asked me to sign them before her all-county cross-country meet last fall, for good luck.

"Sure. We'll do it later," I said, trying to keep my voice light. As much as I wished she would flop back on the bed, turn to the next page of the old September issue, and spill Bugle crumbs everywhere, I was determined not to be the annoying friend.

A pink Post-it fell off the wall and fluttered to the carpet like a leaf off a tree as she turned toward my door. There were leaves all over the ground at the all-county meet, and when Summer ran past me, she left a trail of their fire-colors behind. I'd held my sign straight up in the air, purple with letters written in silver glitter: RUN, SUMMER, RUN.

"Yes. Later. Obviously." She kissed the air. "Love ya."

Each of her footsteps down the stairs punched a new hole in my chest.

"Love ya," I mumbled to the door.

"Not staying for dinner, Summer?" I heard Mom ask from downstairs.

"I can't tonight, Mrs. Martinez, but thank you."

"Stay, stay, stay," my brother Edgar's shrill, two-year-old voice begged. One of his toys played music. Most likely the plush clownfish that sang about life underwater.

Stay, Summer, Stay.

"I'll see you later, Eddie," she said sweetly.

Our front door closed too hard, because Summer didn't know how to do anything softly.

I went to the window and pulled back the curtain. It was blue with clouds printed on it. The clouds were gray instead of white, like my room always held the chance of rain. I watched Summer cross the stretch of grass between my house and hers and disappear through the side door. A minute later she was at her bedroom window, directly across from mine. She looked over at me, waved once, and then her blinds dropped down quick as a blink.

I stepped away from the window and went to my closet. Past my row of dresses and the stacks of shoeboxes was a paper bag from Arthur's General Store. I used most of the brown bags to cover the textbooks teachers assigned us on the first day of school, but not this one. I pulled a small notebook and feather pen from inside. The cover was deep purple suede and the spiral binding was shiny. On the inside, in what Summer had called "the most perfect penmanship" she'd ever seen, I'd written *Lyric Libro*. My lyric book, named in half Spanish and half English, like me.

If I was putting that Elena Recipe together, there would be a secret ingredient. A sprinkle of songwriting.

Writing songs was different from writing papers. I wasn't

trying to get an A. I was catching words that glittered like stars in my head. I thought about writing *music* on my future therapist notepad. A different kind of medicine for broken hearts.

Is there even a cure
For not feeling sure
A way to treat
A slamming door

The rhyme wasn't quite right, but that was okay. I whisper-sang the words, trying to put a melody behind them. My voice was soft even though I wanted to belt out big, beautiful notes, wanted to know if I even could. I'd never tried to sing my songs out loud. Or any song, really. In chorus class, I'd move my mouth without making a sound. It was too scary not knowing what would come out, whether my voice would crack in front of everyone.

I wondered for a second if I should send one of my songs as the writing sample for my Flyers application. But I knew I wouldn't. I'd send the essay I wrote in English class on why I wanted to be a therapist, and keep my Lyric Libro hidden in the paper bag in my closet where no one would ever find it.

my phone looking for someone else to text, someone else to invite over, but there was only her. Being with Summer was smooth sailing. Safe. With anyone else it felt like I was out in rough water, stumbling around and slightly seasick.

"A sonnet." Riah's sneakers tapped the floor under her desk. The white soles were streaked with dirt. I hadn't been able to figure Riah out yet. She wore the kind of clothes that stores put on mannequins in their front windows. The kind of clothes Mom said we could find cheaper somewhere else. But no matter what Riah was wearing she always had her running sneakers on.

"Correct. And what is a line of verse with five metrical feet, each having one unstressed syllable followed by one stressed syllable?"

Iambic pentameter went under *sonnet.* I liked the poetry unit. Poems were a little like songs, but less terrifying. Poems could be tucked away in books, read in quiet. Songs you had to belt out loud. You had to use your voice. And I wasn't as good at using my voice as I was studying the words in my textbooks.

"How about . . . Elena?"

My head shot up and my face burned. I didn't need a mirror to know my cheeks would soon be scarlet. Talking in class was bad enough, but being called on when my hand wasn't up (which it never was) was a different level of nightmare.

"It's. Um. Iambic pentameter. I think."

Chapter
Two

The Extra Credit

One week before summer vacation, I was in language arts listening to Mrs. Parekh go over poetry terms for our final exam.

"What kind of poem often has romantic themes?" she asked us.

I wrote *sonnet* in my notebook. Out of the corner of my eye, I saw a few hands go up.

"Riah?" Mrs. Parekh picked Riah Santangelo. Riah had midnight black hair that touched her shoulder blades. I thought of Summer sprinting out of my room to hang out with her three weeks ago. They'd hung out two more times since then, and each time I'd sit at my desk by the window and wait for Summer to come home, waves of loneliness and pathetic-ness rolling through my chest. I'd scroll through

"You *know*," Mrs. Parekh said, smiling at me the same way she did when she returned my graded tests. I didn't feel like smiling back. I looked down at my page of notes and breathed until the color in my face drained and my heart settled down. Mrs. Parekh asked a few more questions on rhyme schemes, but I stopped copying down the answers. Instead I scribbled small words in the margins, words no one would be able to read but me.

Being called on without warning
Is like a bunch of bees swarming.
Stinging, stinging, stinging
Until I'm bruised.

"Last item on the agenda is extra credit readings. Would anyone like to recite a poem for extra credit today?"

I glanced at my classmates. The readings were part of the poetry unit, and almost everyone else had read a poem for ten points of extra credit. Joey Demarco picked that poem about the wheelbarrow and the chickens and the raindrops, the one that's only eight lines long. Kiki Park read the Robert Frost poem about going down the road less travelled. I decided that's what I was doing in this class. Taking the road where I wouldn't have to speak in front of everyone.

"I'd like to go." Riah raised her hand again. I erased the lyrics I'd written in the margins. I wondered what it was like to be fearless. To be able to stand in front of my classmates without my face catching fire.

"Excellent. What poem will you be reading?"

"'Caged Bird' by Maya Angelou."

Mrs. Parekh nodded and clasped her hands together, then motioned to the head of the room and went to sit in the back. I thought I saw her glance in my direction, but I looked away. Riah made her way to the front, her sneakers squeaking on the floor.

"'A free bird leaps on the back of the wind,'" she began.

Her voice was clear and bright and the words drew me in like a spell. By the time she was done, I felt like I understood that caged bird. Sometimes I felt stuck in my own body, all these songs inside me that I was too scared to let out. *Diagnosis: extreme shyness. Treatment: hide.*

We snapped our fingers when Riah finished, the way Mrs. Parekh had taught us.

"Beautiful," Mrs. Parekh said, and traded places with Riah. When Riah sat at her desk, I could see that her eyes were wet and sparkly. She rubbed a cheek against her T-shirt and tapped her sneakers some more.

The bell to change classes rang. I grinned and stuffed my notebook into my backpack. When I looked at the door, Summer was there, like always, since our language arts classes were next door to each other. The routine of it was enough to make me forget about Mrs. Parekh calling on me. During our unit on *The Outsiders*, Mrs. Parekh had written *I know you know your stuff. I'd love to hear your voice more in class.* in blue pen on the last page of one of my tests. But my mouth stayed shut, my hands writing the answers to her questions in the margin of my notebook instead.

"Elena? Can you stay behind?" Mrs. Parekh asked. The rest of the class filed out. A few of my classmates looked at me like I was in trouble, and my stomach twisted. I'd answered her question. Even with my face red and my palms all sweaty. What had I done wrong? Summer still stood at the door, but Riah was with her now. I went over to Mrs. Parekh.

"If this is about earlier, I'm sorry. I was just caught off guard," I explained.

Mrs. Parekh half smiled. Her skin was warm brown and her kind eyes watched me from behind wire-frame glasses.

"It's not about that." She tilted her head. "Well, actually I suppose it is. You know participation is ten percent of your grade, yes?"

"Sort of." I remembered reading that in her syllabus on the first day of school and crossing it out with my pencil.

"And you know that based on your participation throughout the year that would give you an A minus for a final grade?"

"An A minus?" Just as the panic tore through my chest, I heard laughing from the doorway behind me. When I turned, Summer and Riah had their heads close and their hands clamped over each other's mouths.

"Extra credit would help. Like the poetry reading, for example?"

I forced myself to look away from whatever was happening in the hall, the way it pushed my heart up into my throat, and turned back to Mrs. Parekh.

"An A minus could ruin my chances of being number one in the class," I whispered.

Mrs. Parekh leaned against the radiators that ran along the wall of the classroom.

"Elena, you are so bright. Don't you think the world deserves to hear what you have to say? Because I do."

I didn't know what the world deserved to hear, because the only thing I could hear was Summer laughing out in the hall with Riah. The heavy feeling I'd had when she rushed out of my room settled on my shoulders. *But she came back,* I reminded myself. *Even when they hang out, she always comes back. Up her driveway and the creaky wooden stairs to her bedroom, to her window right across from mine.*

"If I promise to participate more for the next two weeks, can I improve my grade?" I asked.

"I know your grades mean a lot to you. But I want you to participate because you see that you have important things to share with the class. Not to get an A."

"I understand. I really do."

Mrs. Parekh didn't look convinced, but she nodded.

"All right, Elena. You can go. I'm sure you would hate to be late for your next class."

I rushed for the door, ready to spill to Summer about

what Mrs. Parekh had said. But she wasn't there. The hall-way was almost empty. I was alone and late. I dashed down the hall, wishing I was as fast as Summer so I could catch up with her. We only had two classes together this year, gym and earth science. In earth science, we sat on tall stools next to each other at the lab bench, our textbooks sprawled open in front of us like *Spread Your Wings* magazines. One time Mr. Collins asked me about the pH level of soil when my hand wasn't up, and Summer read the answer I'd written in my notebook. She blurted it out before my cheeks could heat up too much, before I could try to stumble through my answer even though it was right there in front of me. Mr. Collins wrinkled his forehead and told her to raise her hand, but when he turned away, Summer just nudged me and smiled.

That's the way it was with Summer. I let her into the textbooks in my brain, all the information I had stored in there. And when I needed it, she'd give me her voice.

Chapter Three

The Pickleball Paddle

I wrinkled my nose at the dirty-laundry-mixed-with-hairspray smell of the girls' locker room and made my way to my spot. Summer was already there. She had changed into a loose red tank top and black leggings. She sat on the bench between the rows of lockers, scrolling through her phone. I dialed my locker combination and took my gym clothes out while I filled her in on what had happened in language arts.

"She's going to Elena-fail you if you don't read a poem in class?" she asked.

Summer knew an A minus was as bad as an F to me.

"Pretty much." I held my clothes against my chest. Around me other girls stripped off their school clothes to change, but I had never been able to change in front of people that easily. Not even Summer.

"Why don't you read Shel Silverstein? Everyone will be laughing too hard at the poem to even notice you," Summer suggested.

"Right. Standing up in front of the class with everyone laughing at me. That's exactly what I want."

Summer smirked and flipped her phone around to show me the screen.

"New strategy. Just ask yourself what Cailin 'Magnet' Carter would do." A picture from Cailin Carter's page was on Summer's phone. She knelt on a striped towel in a yellow bikini, her head leaned back to the sun. The caption said *quick trip to Miami.*

"I wouldn't be in this position if I was Cailin Carter," I said. I saw the little red heart that indicated Summer had liked the picture. "I'd be in Miami on a school day. Wearing sunglasses the size of my face."

Cailin was one of the stars of *On the Mat*, a new six-episode documentary series about Lone Star Elite, the biggest and best cheerleading gym in Dallas, Texas. The first season came out a few months ago. Everyone was watching and posting about it, and especially about Cailin. She was tiny and pretty and perfect and had a little Southern twang in her honey-sweet voice. For the last six weeks Summer and I had watched a new episode every Thursday after school in her sunroom. We loved it even though neither of us had ever been a cheerleader before. And when Cailin fell out of her stunt at the world championships, my heart ached for her as badly as if it were me.

"Two minutes, people," our gym teacher, Ms. Debra, called out from the head of the locker room. Then the door slammed behind her.

"Oops." I took my clothes and sneakers and darted into the shower stall, sliding the curtain closed behind me. If I could just change out there with everyone else, I would have been ready to go. But changing feels just like standing up in front of the class and reading a poem. I'd be exposed. Exposed for my thick legs and the way my soft stomach spilled over my waistband. I pulled my T-shirt and sweat-pants on as fast as I could and then ran out to the gym. I didn't like to spend too long in that small stall. Partly because I didn't want to be late, partly because it smelled like mildew, and partly because of what I'd heard Summer say about me outside the curtain two weeks ago, when she didn't know I was in there.

I found my spot next to Summer where our class was huddled, pushing away all the sad lyrics that filled my head from the memory.

"We're playing pickleball." Ms. Debra had what looked like Ping-Pong equipment in her hand, but the paddle and ball were oversized. "It's tennis but with a paddle instead of a racket."

Ms. Debra started to explain the scoring rules and said

we'd be playing in teams of two. Summer and I stood at the edge of the circle. I saw Kendra Blair and Sara Smith shift closer to us. Kendra and Sara were on cross-country with Summer, but Summer said they spent most of the spring practices sipping out of their Hydro Flasks and talking to the boys on the team. I'd seen a lot of posts on their pages with filters that gave them cat ears and pink noses, but none of the two of them actually running.

They stopped when Kendra was almost shoulder to shoulder with Summer.

"How's it going with your replacement best friend?" Kendra asked.

My head jerked toward Summer and then back to Ms. Debra. She was bouncing the ball on her paddle and motioning for us to try that first, to get used to the feeling.

"Shut up, Kendra," Summer said under her breath.

"Oops, did you not tell Elena yet?" Kendra looked at Sara. She put a hand over her heart and pushed her bottom lip out.

"Aw," Sara added.

Kendra and Sara were the worst kind of duo. They worked together to get under your skin, to make you spew out secrets, smiling the whole time.

"Grab your equipment." Ms. Debra pointed to the crates by her feet, one full of paddles, the other full of rubber balls. Kendra and Sara walked away whispering. Summer didn't move, which made me uneasy, because usually she'd be the first one to make it to the crates. Otherwise we'd get stuck with the cracked paddles.

"What's she talking about?" I asked.

Summer shook her head.

"I don't know. It's Kendra and Sara. Who cares?"

I couldn't help it. I pictured Summer with Riah outside Mrs. Parekh's classroom, their hands over each other's mouths.

"Did she mean Riah?"

Summer's head snapped toward me.

"Seriously, Elena?" She took off toward the crates. I followed behind, nearly tripping over my feet.

"I'm sorry, I'm sorry," I said. "You've just been hanging out with her a lot lately and I didn't even know you were friends." The words fell out. I took a breath and tried to exhale all my clinginess away. Clinginess was like claws digging into Summer's ribs. Clinginess was what made her say those things in the locker room.

We were at the crates. Only a few paddles and balls were left. Summer picked one up. The words *u suck* were scratched into the wood. She put it back in the crate.

"We're on the cross-country team together," Summer said. "Plus, I'm allowed to have other friends. It doesn't mean I'm replacing you."

But I heard what you said in the locker room. The words bubbled up in my throat, but I couldn't say them. Other partners were set up at the nets. The only paddle left was the *u suck* one. I took it.

"Forget Kendra," I said, instead of the things I wanted to. The things that would shine a light on the cracks in our friendship. I'd rather seal them up with superglue. "Be my partner?"

Summer sighed.

"Obviously. But I get to serve first," she said, as if that were really a question.

I handed her the ball and Summer headed over to one side of the net.

The Letter

The noontime sun beamed through my bedroom window the way it does on the first day of summer vacation, bright yellow and full of freedom. I sat at my desk labeling parts of a cell on a worksheet. Mitochondria, nucleus, cytoplasm. A brain is like a bike—if you ignore it too long it'll get rusty.

Something small and solid pinged against my window. I smiled down at the worksheet. When I slid open the cloud curtains, Summer was there at the window across from me. A bag of pebbles for her betta fish's tank sat beside her.

"Let me guess. Homework?" she called out.

"You know I prefer to call it practice in the summer."

"Can Elena take a break to come out and play?" she said jokingly, in a little kid voice. I don't know at what age "playing" switches to "hanging out," but I liked that Summer was the one I'd done it all with.

"Let me just finish this page," I answered.

"It's the first day of vacation!" She took another pebble and tossed it. It hit the side of the house and then dropped to the grass.

"I just have one more. . . ." The sound of rolling tires cut me off. A second later a set of brakes whined with a *screech*. Roll, *screech*. Roll, *screech*. Summer and I gave one frantic glance at each other and then burst away from our windows. *The mail was here.*

I took off down the stairs, skipping the bottom three steps with a big jump. I landed on the *Bienvenidos* mat in the doorway.

"Nice moves, Lenny. What's the rush?"

I turned toward my dad's voice. He was in the living room kneeling on the carpet in the blue suit he wore for open houses, prying the remote from Edgar's small fist, his black hair gleaming with gel. Mom sat on the couch with Edgar's plush clownfish. She wore her scrubs with the crayons on them and her caramel-colored hair was tied up. When I was born, my hair was light and wispy like hers. The baby pictures on our mantel were proof. But as I got older it turned dark and curly like Dad's and his mom's, my abuelita.

"The mail's here," I said. I opened the front door. Now just the screen stood between me and Summer and the letter from *Spread Your Wings*. If it was even in there. The instructions said we would find out by the end of June.

"So *that's* what it takes to tear you away from your books. A mail truck. Not your old dad coming home to eat lunch with you on the first day of summer." He turned the volume on the TV down. Little blue mice danced around on the screen. "What do you think, Eddie? Should I leave the Realtor life and join the postal service?"

"I push," Edgar whined. He reached for the remote.

"Edgar, what about Fishy?" Mom asked, and made the clownfish dance on the couch.

The sound of the tires got closer. I looked through the screen. The truck was at the Goldbergs' whale-shaped mailbox next door, where Summer was standing. The mail carrier handed her a stack of letters and then drove slowly on to our mailbox. Summer looked in my direction, waving her arms like she was trying to get my attention in a big crowd.

"Sorry, Dad." I darted barefoot out the door. My legs were shaky as the wind zipped in my ears. Summer was jumping up and down now, wearing a white tank top, hot pink bike shorts, and her sneakers with my good luck signature.

"It's here!" she screamed. She plucked an envelope out of the stack and dumped the rest into the daffodils by her feet. I made it to my mailbox, my breath coming in quick spurts from the running and the nerves. Summer told me once that on good runs it felt like she could keep going forever, just her and her sneakers pounding against the ground. But I could never go too far without stopping.

I paused with my hand on the black metal mail flap.

"Elena, what are you doing? It's here," she said. She shook the cream-colored envelope at me.

"I'm too nervous," I replied. I couldn't make my hand move. Summer came closer and held the mailbox with me.

"Together, then," she said. She smelled like her Sport Strength deodorant, a soapy shower-fresh scent. Summer tugged harder than me when we opened my mailbox, but it felt better to have her there. I flipped through the catalog for Mom and the credit card bill for Dad and the advertisement from the grocery store for *Resident*. There at the bottom of the stack was the square envelope with the *Spread Your Wings* logo in the corner. The beige color reminded me of sand, and a set of wings was drawn at the tip of the flap. I squeezed the letter tight like it might fly away.

Summer and I faced each other. Our envelopes were the same size and shape, and in my heart I knew that meant what was inside must be the same too. I'd read once on a college message board that acceptance letters and rejection letters looked different. My stomach squirmed like it did before a big test, or when Mom made me small-talk with relatives.

"On three?" I asked.

Summer nodded.

"One, two . . . ," she started.

"Three."

I dug my finger under the flap and tore it open, my hands too shaky to be careful about it. The top of the envelope turned jagged like teeth. I pulled out the letter, letting the envelope fall to the ground. The paper was folded. I looked up and saw that Summer was already reading hers, ahead of me like always. I looked down.

Congratulations, Elena. You have been chosen as a Flyer for the September issue of Spread Your Wings*!*

"Ahh!" I squealed like an animal on one of Edgar's cartoons. Like a person can only squeal when something so blissfully amazing happens you don't care what you sound like. My heart was pounding when I closed the space between Summer and me and wrapped my arms around her neck. "Summer! We're going to be Flyers!"

Summer was stiff. Her arms didn't loop around me. They hung limp by her sides. When I looked down I could see the letter pinched between her fingers, my name in cursive peeking out from the side of her shoe.

"I didn't get picked," she mumbled. I pulled back and held my own letter tighter.

"What?"

"I. Didn't. Get. Picked." I'd never heard her words sound that way before. They were slow and enunciated. Broken-glass sharp. She dropped her letter into the daffodils with the rest of her mail.

"Oh," I said.

My head spun like when I learned something big and new, but when it was school the information would straighten out with enough studying. I didn't see how this would ever make sense. Summer's face was pink, her freckles like angry orange splotches, her mouth a hard-set line.

"I'm so happy for you, Elena." But she didn't sound happy for me, and she didn't look happy. A breeze too chilly for the end of June blew by. "Read me your letter."

Diagnosis: only half of a dream coming true. Treatment: act like it's not coming true at all.

"No, that's okay," I said.

"Don't do that. Don't downplay yourself like you always do." I tried not to notice how harsh her voice sounded on the "always." "Read it to me."

I lifted my letter.

"'Congratulations, Elena. You have been chosen as a Flyer for the September issue of *Spread Your Wings*! We can't wait to see you in New York City. Your fellow Flyers will be Whitney Richards, eleven, Harlow Yoshida, twelve, and Cailin Carter, thirteen. We have set up a virtual chat for you all to get acquainted before your arrival. You will be . . .'"

"Cailin Carter? Like, from *On the Mat*?" Summer asked, eyes wide.

"I'm sure it's not," I said. Because if it was *that* Cailin, there was no way I should have been picked. Cailin Carter was a celebrity. And I did parts-of-a-cell worksheets during summer vacation.

"Keep going," Summer said. The storminess in her face was starting to pass but not enough for me to be sure we'd be okay. And I *needed* us to be okay. I needed to know there'd be more days of watching TV in her sunroom, more pebbles tossed at each other's windows. I'd held on to those small moments so tightly lately, desperate not to let the distance between us grow wider.

"'The program will begin with your arrival on Sunday, July twelfth, and conclude on Friday, July seventeenth. You will help the *Spread Your Wings* staff put together the issue, spend time developing your writing, and, of course, explore the city.'" I skipped a whole paragraph about travel arrangements. My throat was too dry to read much more. "'We can't wait to meet you. Fly high, The *Spread Your Wings* Internship Team.'"

Summer kicked some of the soil around the daffodils. Dust covered the spot on her sneaker where my signature was.

"That's amazing," she said softly.

"I'm not going to go."

Her head shot up.

"You are absolutely going, Elena Martinez."

"That's only two weeks away. I just don't see how . . ."

She put her hands on my shoulders and squeezed.

"You are going if I have to pull you there by your ponytail.

You are going if I have to pack you in a box and mail you to New York." She looked down at me, her green eyes fierce under her long orange eyelashes.

I laughed and it felt like relief. But New York was a hundred miles away from Franklin City. How could I keep Summer close with all that space between us?

"Can I pack you in a box and bring you with me?"

She rolled her eyes and smiled a little.

"Obviously."

Over her shoulder I saw someone coming down the street. She wore paisley print leggings and had her jet-black hair in a messy bun. Riah. I pictured the glimmer of tears in her eyes after she read "Caged Bird." Summer noticed my focus had shifted and turned around. She checked her watch, the one that told her the time and her heart rate and how fast she was running, and grinned. The Truly Happy Dimple appeared.

"You're early," she called out to Riah.

"I couldn't wait anymore." Riah jogged the rest of the way over to us and her bun swayed. "Hey, Elena."

"Hi," I said, but it came out like a croak. My cheeks flushed. I glanced at Summer. Her face was lit up like when a new issue of *Spread Your Wings* came. A crack split through my chest. What if she never looked at the magazine the same way again?

"We're going for a run," Summer explained. She kicked

her leg back, grabbed her ankle, and tugged into a stretch.

"Do you want to come?" Riah asked.

The heat in my face deepened.

"Um . . . well . . . I don't really . . ." I waited for Summer to finish my sentence. Her eyes flicked toward me, fast and aggravated, like this time she didn't want to. I was being *that* friend again, the friend who stuck like gum to the bottom of a shoe.

"Elena doesn't run."

In that moment I wished I could trade my textbooks for a track, my studying for sneakers. Anything to keep Summer in stride with me.

"We can go slow," Riah suggested.

I knew every look on Summer's face the way I knew the parts of a cell. Wrinkled forehead, narrow eyes, lips rolled together. Her *can we not?* look.

"It's okay," I said, staring at the ground. "My dad came home to have lunch with me."

"Fun!" Riah ran in place. She faced Summer. "Ready?"

Summer nodded and they both turned around, toward the top of Daybury Street, then started to jog.

"Talk to you later?" I called out before Summer got too far.

"Sure," she answered without turning her head back.

I watched them until they disappeared, imagining they were off to take Summer's favorite route. I always thought of it as our route, and when we took it together we would walk, not run. It wound through the woods and ended up on a street near the water, where there were big gray beach houses shaped like wrapped packages. We could get to the Franklin City Boat Launch by climbing over the stone wall, and we'd walk across the kelpy sand to sit on the dock. People would set up their boats and take off, names like *Princess Tiffany II* and *Sea Crusher* painted on the sides.

"Let's sail away some day. Just the two of us," Summer said when we first found the route. We were sitting with our legs dangling over the blue-green water.

"I've never heard a more perfect plan," I'd answered. Because of course I'd go anywhere if it could be just us. It was better that way. I imagined our own boat, the *Sum-lena*, headed straight for where the sun met the water.

I hoped with all my heart that she and Riah weren't going there.

The walk to my front door was different from when I rushed out. I could feel the sharp grass bite my feet. Summer was gone. And I had a letter in my hand that said I was supposed to be a Flyer.

"Fill us in!" Mom said when I was back on the *Bienvenidos* mat. The cartoon mice were still dancing on the TV like the whole world hadn't changed. Dad looked at me, pretending to nervously bite his nails.

"In a minute." I climbed the stairs and closed my bedroom door behind me. I left the Flyer letter on my comforter and went to the closet. The letter sat next to me when I returned, still and patient, while I opened my Lyric Libro.

A teardrop splattered between the lines on the blank page. It seeped in and spread wide. I tried to stop the aching feeling in my chest. My dream had come true. But it had come true without Summer. The facts were opposites, protons and electrons, and my brain didn't know how to make them coexist.

When I was a therapist, I would be taught to understand how people could be happy and sad at once. I would help them decipher the things that hurt. Answer their hardest questions.

I pulled the feather pen out of the paper bag and started to write.

Please don't run so far I can't catch you,
Off to places I don't know how to get to.
Don't you know that if I could
I'd keep you with me.

FLYERS CHAT

Whitney R.:

Okay I need to get this chat started RIGHT NOW because I am TOO EXCITED!

Harlow Y.:

I was about five minutes from starting it myself, so I appreciate your gumption.

Whitney R.:

Gumption? GREAT word!

Harlow Y.:

My journalism teacher tells me I should vary my word choice.

Cailin C.:

That's good advice cause otherwise we'd all be going around just saying cool and good and nice all the time.

Whitney R.:

Hey, I have NOTHING against the word "cool."

Harlow J.:

My journalism teacher would probably tell me to use "invigorating."

Cailin C.:

How invigorating is my new sweater?

Whitney R.:

How INVIGORATING is it that we're going to be in a
MAGAZINE?!?

Harlow Y.:

Where is our other invigorating Flyer, Elena?

Cailin C.:

Yeah, Elena, are you there?

Whitney R:

We want to MEET you!

Harlow Y.:

I think we might have scared her. Or as my journalism
teacher would probably suggest, she's "petrified."

The Stars

Thursday was movie night in the Martinez house. Mom made two bowls of popcorn—one with just butter for Dad and Edgar and one covered in black pepper and parmesan for her and me. Dad said our combination was a crime against popcorn, which just made Mom and me dig our hands deeper into our special bowl and laugh.

"What should we put on?" Mom asked. She walked in from the kitchen with the two plastic green bowls, then gave one to Dad.

"Let's let Elena pick. It's a special night for her," he suggested.

I was on the couch, pulling at a loose thread on the blue corduroy cushion.

"Why?" Edgar asked. He plopped butt-first onto the

carpet, his plush clownfish in his hands.

"Your sister is going to help make a magazine." Mom smiled at me. "Tell us more about it, Lenny."

The thread snapped off in my hand. I let it fall to the rug. That afternoon I'd read the letter ten times, scoured every inch of the *Spread Your Wings* website for information about past Flyers' experiences. Maybe I had pages from the magazine pasted all over my wall, but I had no idea what it meant to be part of it. I only knew the pictures of the Flyers on their trips to Central Park and the Museum of Ice Cream, the essays they'd write at the end. I didn't know what it would feel like to be there. How the days would go. How I would get through it without Summer.

"We visit places around the city. We help write some of the features. And if you like photography or fashion or production you get to help with that. It's like magazine camp, I guess."

"What part of the magazine do you think you'll be helping with?" Dad wrestled Edgar into his arms. "I can give you some fashion tips if you need them." He tossed his head back like a model.

Edgar laughed, but I couldn't. My heart felt all locked up. Nowhere on the *Spread Your Wings* website did it explain what a secret songwriter with good grades and red cheeks could possibly bring to the pages of the magazine.

"Can we just watch the movie?" I asked, leaning my head

back against the couch. My parents glanced at each other.

"Sure. Pick one," Mom said.

"Fish!" Edgar screamed.

"No, not again, Eddie," Dad said.

"It doesn't matter to me. We can watch the fish movie," I said.

"No. We can't. I've started seeing clownfish in my dreams." Dad jokingly squeezed both sides of his head and clenched his teeth.

"Fine. Let's watch the dancing one. We all like that one," I said. Dad undid his funny face and nodded slowly before scooting toward the movie cabinet under the TV, Edgar still in his lap.

"Are you all right, Lenny? I would've expected you to be a little happier about all this," Mom asked.

"I am happy," I replied, deadpan.

"Sad," Edgar chimed in. He tossed movie cases to the side while Dad searched, the plush clownfish in his mouth now.

"Thanks, Eddie." I rolled my eyes.

"Does this have anything to do with you getting picked and not Summer?" Mom handed me the popcorn bowl. She always did that. When she asked me something hard, she'd pass over a piece of chocolate or the remote or her hand. Something for me to hold on to. But I pushed the bowl away this time.

"No, I just don't think I should go. I need to be here to babysit Edgar."

"It's only for a week, hon. We'll be fine."

I looked down. I moved my pinkie nail over my checkered pajama pants, writing invisible lyrics.

"Lenny." Dad was closer to the couch now. The Blu-ray case was open in his hand, and the disc flashed with rainbow colors from the lamplight. I didn't answer. "It might be good for you to do this on your own. You don't always need Summer there next to you."

"I said that's not what this is about!"

Edgar dropped his clownfish and it started to sing its song. All my feelings burst inside me like popcorn kernels. Deep lines formed in Dad's forehead when he frowned. I'd never yelled at him before. I'd never yelled at *anyone* before. Not even when Edgar finger-painted on my math homework.

"Okay. Let's watch the movie. We'll talk about this later," Mom said.

Ten minutes into the movie Edgar fell asleep on the rug. I sat on the couch with Mom, the bowl of popcorn between us. She kept glancing at me in the dark as if I wouldn't see her. I curled my legs up to my chest and focused on breathing until the credits rolled.

Around midnight, I was wide-awake in bed when I heard the taps against my window. At first, I thought I'd imagined it. I squeezed my eyes shut and tried not to think about burglars breaking in. The sharp ping came again, louder this time.

I unburied myself from the covers and crossed the carpet to my desk. Summer was at her window. The only light came from the lamp on the side table next to her. She kept her cross-country medals there. I slid my window open.

"You're up late," I said.

Summer hardly ever stayed up late, because she liked to wake up early. Even when we had sleepovers. One time, I woke up at her house and her side of the bed was empty. She stood at her window with her hands on the sill, staring.

"What are you doing?" I asked.

"Watching the sunrise." She looked at me and her face was half shadow, half light. "Come watch too."

"But I'm so comfortable," I whined, and tugged Summer's sheet up to my chin. It smelled like her.

"Sometimes you have to get uncomfortable or you'll never experience things!" she whisper-shouted.

I surrendered and climbed out of the bed. My eyes were still heavy with sleep, but I went to stand with her at the window. Outside was my house, and the tips of the spiky pine trees surrounding our yards. Above it all the sky turned pink and blue. A few stars still hung up there, softly glowing.

"It would've been sad to miss this," I said.

"Told you so."

I tried a few times after that to wake up for the sunrise.

But sometimes I overslept. Or I was too busy getting ready for school to notice it. Or I was just so warm in my bed I couldn't make it to the window.

"I can't sleep," Summer said. "I feel too terrible."

"About what?" My mind replayed the sound of Summer's sharp voice in the driveway, the image of her and Riah running away. But in this moment I wanted to super-stretch my arms out to Summer's window and make her feel better.

"How I was acting earlier. I was jealous and being the worst friend. You never would have been like that if I got in and you didn't."

"I wish it had happened that way," I said. My voice cracked.

"I don't. I really am so, so happy for you, Elena. And I know you're scared, but you're going to be amazing."

Sometimes you have to get uncomfortable or you'll never experience things.

I looked up at the sky. The stars sparkled like guiding lights. Maybe if I kept my head up and my eyes on them, I would end up right where I was supposed to be. I felt patched up, like there was gauze wrapped around all the wounds from earlier. I wouldn't have to do this big thing with Summer mad at me. Because we *were* still friends, no matter what had happened this year.

"I'll text you the whole time," I said.

Summer's laugh filled up the darkness.

"I know."

pencil box on my desk had stones inside. I took one out and drew my arm back, ready to toss it across the yard to Summer's window. She would tell me to press the button. Her words would be fast and firm, and it would be exactly what I needed to settle my nerves. On the first day of sixth grade, Summer and I got off the bus and stood together in front of Franklin City Middle School. She reached out to grab my wrist, and her fingers grazed the pulse point.

"Elena, your heart is racing!" she said.

The door on the bus squealed when it closed.

"Yeah, I'm freaking out." In my head the windows on the build-ing turned to monster eyes, the doors a mouth full of sharp teeth.

"It's going to be great," Summer said, and let go of my wrist. "Don't worry."

Her assurance had made me feel better then, smoothed my heartbeat out. But now it made me feel kind of nauseous. I dropped the stone back into the pencil box. Across the yard Summer's white lace curtains were closed. She couldn't take care of everything this time. She wasn't going to be a Flyer. I was.

The laptop chimed again. I went to sit on the bed and brought the screen back to life. The message reappeared. *Are you ready to submit?*

I dropped my hand to the trackpad, paused for one more second.

Treatment: just do it.

Chapter
Six
—

The Send Button

The laptop on my bed chimed and went dark for the fifth time. I sighed, wiggling my finger on the track pad until it lit up again. A message from the *Spread Your Wings* site waited on the screen, where it had been for the past hour, blinking and bright purple and asking if I was ready to submit. I'd clicked the button that said I was accepting my Flyer position. The permission slips and emergency contact information sheets were signed by my parents and uploaded. All I had to do was press send. My hand hovered above the computer, and each time it lowered down, I pulled back like the keyboard might burn me.

Diagnosis: that moment right before you do something big when you convince yourself you can't.

I got up and walked to the window. The zebra-print

Chapter
Seven

The Train Station

I had been to Grand Central Station twice before, one time on a class field trip to the Met and the other with my family, Summer, and her parents during the holidays. The train station feels like two different worlds. One minute you're in a dim tunnel, surrounded on all sides by other passengers getting off the train. The walls and ceiling are cement, and the tracks look broken, and sometimes a rat crawls out from underneath the platform. But then you keep walking and the space opens up to a lobby that looks more like a museum than a train station. Marble staircases spiral up on each side. Painted constellations cover the ceiling. A Taurus bull charges with its horns down across the teal-blue sky, and the Cancer crab crawls into the corner. I feel like I have a personal connection with the station because Mom reads our horoscope online every morning. We're both Cancers.

"Cancer, July twelfth. You will find an opportunity to be adventurous today. Although not second nature to you, you should seize the opportunity. You may surprise yourself," she read from her phone after we parked outside the train station in Franklin City.

"You're making that up," I said. *I wrung the handle of the duffel bag at my feet.*

"Prove it." *She smiled at me and snuck the phone back into the pocket of her purple scrubs.*

I looked up at the starry Cancer crab now. I followed the direction of its claws off to the side of the main terminal, near a staircase, to call Mom and let her know I'd gotten here safe. And even though the train station felt enormous, and it was loud, and I didn't have the seventh-grade class or my family or Summer here, the excitement gripped me. I was going to be a Flyer. I almost burst out singing.

Against all odds I'm standing here.

All this joy leaves no room for fear.

A sound cut through the commotion around me. Loud, shallow, crackling breaths. I looked away from my phone. A girl my age sat on the stairs next to a purple duffel bag. She had brown tortoiseshell glasses and big, fluffy curls and a hand pressed over her heart. Her shoulders rose and fell too fast, her brown skin shining with sweat.

"Are you okay?" I asked her.

The girl kept breathing and squeezed her eyes shut.

"Panic. Attack," she wheezed.

I looked around for an adult nearby but no one else was paying attention. Passengers rushed up and down the stairs fast, nearly kicking her duffel bag. I looked closer at the embroidery on the bag and saw the familiar cursive writing: *Spread Your Wings*. The same duffel bag Summer and I bought with our Edgar-babysitting money. The same duffel bag slung over my shoulder right now.

I didn't know what to say next, because I never knew what to say, so I put my duffel bag on the stair with the embroidery facing her and hoped she might open her eyes. Maybe seeing we were both *Spread Your Wings* fans would help one breath come easier. I sat down on the step in front of her, next to my bag.

"Can you hold my hand?" The girl held out her hand, and I could see she was shaking from her wrist to her fingers.

"Um. Yes. Sure," I said, and wrapped my hand around hers. Her palm was clammy. I felt the trembling under her skin.

We sat in quiet for a minute. I watched her shoulders stop shaking, listened to her jagged breath get smoother. She took one more big gulp of air and then let it out. It reminded me of runner's breath, which Summer had told me about. She said when she was struggling to take in air during a long run, she would focus on breathing in through her nose and out through her mouth until her lungs calmed down. I thought I should tell the girl about the technique, but maybe someone had already told her about it. Or maybe she wouldn't want to hear it. People have their own ways of getting through things.

She let go of my hand.

"Thank you." She took a tissue from the side pocket of her bag, then took off her glasses to dab at her eyes. "I felt okay the whole ride from Philadelphia. It came out of nowhere. Well, it always does."

"This happens to you a lot?" I asked.

The girl cleared the fog from her glasses and put them back on.

"It happens enough. I mean, even *once* is enough. And it's always at the worst time in the worst place."

Was this where I should mention the runner's breath? Or the matching duffel bags? Words flowed so much easier when it was me and Summer. They flowed easier into my Lyric Libro, too. But this was a stranger. Color flooded to my face.

"I'm Whitney, by the way," she said. "I'd shake your hand but I think we covered that." I was happy to hear her laugh, a soft and twinkly sound. Almost as if she hadn't been breathing so hard a second ago.

Of course. I should've said my name.

"Elena," I said.

Whitney's eyes narrowed, and she shifted her gaze to our duffel bags. Back and forth between the two, once and then again.

"Like Elena Martinez?!" She stood up and stomped her foot. It was funny, because people usually stomp when they're mad, but it seemed like she was doing it to pack even more power into her words. Her curls bounced.

"That's me," I said.

"I'm Whitney *Richards*. We're both Flyers!"

Whitney wore a jean skirt and brown, strappy sandals. Her pink shirt was flowy on top and cinched at her waist. She had a ring on every finger of her left hand, shaped like gold pyramids.

"Wow," was all I could think to say, about her picture-perfect outfit and the coincidence of running into each other. Whitney reached down to pick up her bag.

"It's nice to officially meet. We never heard from you in the group chat." She started walking down the steps and I followed her. I looked up to the Cancer crab, begging the crustacean to help me be brave, seize the opportunity, feel adventurous. Show me how to make friends.

"Yeah, I was having technical difficulties with my phone."

It was a lie, and after the words tumbled out of my mouth, I didn't know why I said it. Whitney turned to look at me. Her jaw dropped.

"How do you even *live*?" she asked.

In a shell. Like a crab.

I wanted to sweep the moment aside and get as far away from the lie as possible. Whitney and I walked across the terminal.

"Do you know where you're going?" I asked.

"No." Whitney giggled. "I was hoping you did."

Being lost seemed like the kind of thing that might make Whitney panic again, which I didn't want to happen now, right in the middle of Grand Central underneath Orion.

"I think the info packet said we should meet our driver at Forty-Second and Lexington." I looked around the terminal. Tunnels veered off in different directions, and there were street names written over the arched doorways in black letters. "There."

I pointed and Whitney squealed.

"I am *so* glad we found each other. Best panic attack ever," she said. We started walking again and I felt something nudge at me. I had helped someone.

"Me too," I said.

Maybe I could do this.

The Tappiston Hotel

The ceilings in the Tappiston Hotel lobby were high with crystal chandeliers, and green plants grew out of white wooden barrels. A seating area near the check-in desk had yellow wicker furniture and the words WELCOME TO THE TAPPISTON written in pink neon lights on a wall made of logs.

"Is it weird to say I want to marry a lobby? Because I want to marry this lobby," Whitney said after we got through the gold revolving doors. The sound of honking horns faded, replaced by soft piano music, and the car-exhaust smell of the city was overpowered by vanilla and roses.

"Not weird," I said. The lobby was the perfect blend of a royal castle and a cozy cabin in the woods. It felt homey even though it was so big.

A girl who looked college-aged crossed the lobby with her gaze set on us. She wore dark jeans and cowboy boots and a shirt with the balloon house from the movie *Up* on it. Her pumpkin-orange hair was tied in a ballerina bun.

"Whitney Richards and Elena Martinez? Are you Whitney and Elena?" she asked when she stopped in front of us. The stack of photos in her hands fell to the floor. I knelt to help her pick them up and saw one was a picture of me in a silver dress at the winter dance, fake snow in my hair. I'd used the picture for my Flyers application. There was a pink Post-it with my name in loopy script stuck on. I thought of the *Spread Your Wings* wall in my room and for a second missed Summer so much it hurt.

"We're Whitney and Elena," I said, and handed her the pictures. The one on top, with the Post-it that said *Cailin,* looked all too familiar. The girl knelt on a striped towel. The sun shone on her face. Her sunglasses were huge.

"Excellent. Thank you. I'm Mindy O'Grady." She took the photos out of my hand and stuffed them into the bag on her shoulder, a beach tote with the words *You've Got a Friend in Me* written in sequins.

Mindy pushed down the frizz around her temples. She talked fast like Summer did, but it was different. It was nervous-sounding and made me feel like I was late for a test no one told me about.

"You work at *Spread Your Wings*?" Whitney asked. She bounced up and down on her toes.

"No. I'm just carrying your pictures around. Ha!" Her fake laugh was loud and made Whitney and me take a step back. "Kidding. Yes. I'm an intern. And your chaperone."

"Ooo-kay then," Whitney mumbled.

I heard the whir of the revolving doors and turned around. Cailin Carter walked in. She wore the same sunglasses from her Miami photo, even though it was early evening and not that bright. Her phone was pressed to her cheek.

"Oh my gosh, it's actually her."

The words slipped from my mouth. Cailin Carter had walked out of Summer's TV right into the Tappiston Hotel lobby in black flip-flops and a tank top that said *Lone Star Elite* inside a red cheerleading bow. She dragged a leopard print suitcase behind her.

"Over here, Cailin!" Whitney called out like it was no big deal.

Cailin smiled tightly and held up her hand. She came to stand on the other side of me, so now I was between her and Whitney.

"*Yes*, Mom, I posted." I noticed her voice was different than on TV; the Southern accent was there, but the sugary tone wasn't. "I asked someone in baggage claim to take it. Mom, I'm at the hotel now, I have to go." She hung up and stuck the phone in her back pocket. Her cheek was pink where the phone had been, like she'd pushed it too hard into her skin.

"Welcome, Cailin. This is Whitney and Elena." Mindy fished through her bag and pulled out a wrinkled packet of paper.

Cailin lifted her sunglasses and looked up at me. She was a few inches shorter than I was. Thick mascara clumped on her eyelashes.

"Hey," she said, as if she didn't have hundreds of thousands of followers, as if Summer and I didn't look at her pictures and ask, *What would Cailin Carter do?*

I opened my mouth but no sound came out. Cailin narrowed her eyes and turned back to Mindy while my face flamed and my chest squeezed. I looked up at the ceiling. There were no stars up there, painted or real. Why was I here? *How* was I here? My crab shell hardened around me.

"Now we're just missing . . . ," Mindy started to say.

"Harlow Yoshida is here!" A flash of black hair came through the revolving doors to stand in our line. She had a beige canvas backpack, a New York Yankees T-shirt, and a pencil behind her ear. "Sorry I'm late. My brother drove me and he's a stupid dumb stupidface."

"Would your journalism teacher approve of that word choice?" Whitney asked.

The three of them laughed at the inside joke I'd seen in the Flyers chat but wasn't a part of.

"In Denny's case, yes," Harlow said. She was small like Cailin and had the bottoms of her jeans rolled up twice. Her eyes were dark like her hair.

"Don't worry, Harlow, you've just completely derailed us. Ha!" Mindy shook her packet and the laughing stopped. "Kidding. Follow me."

Mindy led us toward the wicker seats. Guests milled around, their shoes squeaking on the shiny tile floors. The elevator nearby dinged. All the people and sounds blended together until I was dizzy. *Diagnosis: feeling like a balloon not tied to anything. Treatment: do something to keep your feet on the ground.*

I thought about texting Summer, but there was no time to take my phone out. We sat in a row on a chaise lounge the color of sunflowers.

"Here's the deal. You're in for the night." Mindy flipped a page in her stapled packet. "You can head up to your room and settle in and unpack. Order as much room service as you want. I'll be staying in the hotel too, a few rooms down, if you need anything. Try not to need anything. Ha! Kidding. Here are your room keys."

She handed each of us a plastic card. *Tappiston* was written on them in navy blue letters.

"We can't do *anything* tonight?" Whitney asked. She pressed her room key between her palms like she was praying.

"You can get to know each other." Mindy flicked through her packet of paper one more time. "All right, that's it. Room is on the sixth floor. Giddyup!"

Mindy kicked her leg out, and one of her cowboy boots came flying off, landing with a hollow thud by a potted plant.

The walls of our hotel room were painted ombré brown, lighter on top and darker toward the hardwood floor. There was a ceiling fan with blades shaped like palm tree leaves, and two beds with bamboo headboards and green satin sheets.

"It looks like we'll be cohabitating," Harlow said. She dumped her backpack onto the bed closest to the door.

"Fun!" Whitney jumped, her curls flying with her, as she landed on the other bed.

"What if someone thrashes around in their sleep?" Cailin asked. She lifted her phone and scanned it across the room like she was taking a video. The case had red and black rhinestones. I pressed myself into the corner to get out of view.

"Do *you*?" Harlow asked. She crossed her legs up on the bed. Her hair was pin straight and her cheekbones were sharp. An article in *Spread Your Wings* last month had shown readers how to make your cheeks look like that with strategically placed bronzer, but Harlow didn't have any makeup on.

"I've been told I cheerlead in my sleep. There's no proof though." Cailin pressed her finger into the phone screen.

"They probably would have caught that on camera," Harlow said.

Cailin flinched like someone had slapped her. I thought of her face on episode six of *On the Mat*, right after the world championship performance where her stunt had crumbled to the ground. She placed her phone on the dresser nearby and rolled her lips together.

"They didn't film us while we were sleeping," she said, her voice low. I wasn't able to read the look in her eyes. But it was clear the show was the last thing she wanted to talk about.

"What about you, Elena? Any weird sleeping habits?" Whitney asked. Everyone turned to look at me, flattened against the wall.

I shook my head.

"I call Elena then." Whitney tapped the mattress. I crossed the room, dropping my duffel on the floor. I slid onto the bed next to Whitney. Cailin laid her suitcase on the floor and unzipped it. There were tank tops and jeans folded up next to rolled pairs of socks. I don't know what I was expecting her suitcase to look like, but I didn't think it would be so *normal*.

The room was quiet for a second, other than the whir of the ceiling fan above us. I turned to face the window. Our view looked out to a tall building across the street, made of granite and glass. The light outside was fading gold. I thought about Summer and our windows across from each other. If I threw a pebble out to the other building, who would answer?

"We should do something." Whitney lay back. She tapped her feet against the bed. Her toenails were painted pink and her sandals had at least five buckles on the straps. They looked intricate and stylish like the rest of her outfit.

"Mindy said we couldn't," Cailin reminded her. She slid a drawer open and put her stack of shorts inside.

"Mindy . . ." Whitney trailed off. "I don't know. Give me a word, Harlow."

"Loves Disney?" Harlow suggested.

"That's two words."

"Should come with a warning." Cailin closed the drawer. She picked up the thick black book on the dresser with the room service menu inside.

"That's *five* words!"

Baffling. Fanatical. Hurried. I'd gotten a hundred on every vocabulary test I'd taken since kindergarten. But I couldn't get my mouth to open and my voice to speak up. My mind flashed to an article in *Spread Your Wings* on how to make friends. Tip #3 was to realize that everyone else is just as nervous as you when meeting new people. But Tip #3 obviously hadn't factored in Whitney, Cailin, and Harlow, who were acting like they'd known each other forever.

"Let's go to the pool." Cailin showed us one of the plastic pages in the book. "It's on the second floor."

"I'm in," Harlow said.

"Me too!" Whitney slid her sandals back on and headed for the door. She turned to look at me. "You're coming, right?"

Mom was definitely lying about my horoscope. It wasn't a day to seize adventure. It was a day to be exactly who I was. And who I was did not fit in with exploring hotel pools.

"I have to make a call," I said.

The three of them looked at each other and shrugged. The door closed hard when they left. I sat on the edge of the bed, staring down at the phone in my lap. Tears pricked the back of my eyes and my heart was heavy. Even my hands felt heavy when I unlocked the screen and dialed.

"Hello?" Summer answered after three rings. Her voice sounded like home.

"I can't do this, Summer." My voice shook.

"Is it going badly?" she asked. I could hear her TV on in the background. I closed my eyes and pretended that I was in her sunroom, the stars popping up in the sky through the sliding glass doors.

"I shouldn't be here. There's this girl who dresses so perfectly it's like she stepped out of, well, a magazine, and another who always has something smart and funny to say, and the other is literally Cailin Carter. Like, *that* Cailin Carter."

Summer gasped.

"No way, is she amazing? Tell me she's amazing," she said, brushing past my words like an opponent in one of her races. I sighed.

"I don't know."

"Then get to know her! You can do this. You just have to try." Summer's voice got quieter like she'd moved her head away from the phone. "It's Elena. She's not happy in New York."

My skin burned.

"Don't tell your parents that, they'll tell mine!"

"It's not my parents, I'm at Riah's."

Away from the speaker I heard Riah ask, "Why isn't she happy?" The image I had of Summer sitting in her sunroom, with my house next door and the stars, disappeared. I'd never been to Riah's house. I couldn't picture anything except the two of them next to each other.

"Hi, Riah," I mumbled.

"I'll talk to you tomorrow, okay? Go have fun with Cailin Carter!"

She hung up before I could say bye. I dropped my phone onto the silky comforter and squeezed the fabric between my fingers. Summer's and Riah's voices echoed in my head, muffled, pulled away from the receiver. Like I wasn't supposed to hear what they were saying even though they were talking about me.

I reached into my duffel bag until I found the purple sweatshirt and unraveled my Lyric Libro from inside the big front pocket. The cover was soft and familiar, and the feather pen stuck out of the spine. I flipped back to an earlier page, to a verse I'd written a few weeks ago. After I overheard Summer in the locker room. My mouth formed the words while my hand moved, singing along.

I heard what you said about me today.
I'd never say those things about you.
But I think the very worst part of it all
Is that every word was true.

Chapter
Nine

The Locker Room

Lunch had become my sigh of relief. It was thirty minutes of Summer time, outside of class, just the two of us. After algebra I found Summer at the end of a table in the center of the cafeteria. She waved me over, the sleeve of her burgundy cardigan sliding down.

"Long time no see," Summer said when I sat down. She handed me a baby carrot.

"It really does feel like it's been an eternity," I answered. I chewed the carrot while I unpacked my own lunch from a brown paper bag.

"So dramatic."

A piece of carrot got stuck in my throat. I coughed and my eyes filled up.

"I'm kidding," I said, even though I wasn't.

Summer's gaze moved to a spot over my shoulder. She smiled

*and waved. I turned around and saw Kendra and Sara beckoning
her to their table, smiling with their teeth showing.*

*"Maybe we should go sit with them," Summer suggested. "So
many people sit at their table. Well, all the popular people."*

*There were boys at their table, boys like Joey Demarco and
Grayson Pilsner.*

*"But they're so . . . intimidating," I said. "Remember Joey's
Halloween party?"*

Summer glared at me.

"What is that supposed to mean?"

My heart sputtered.

"Nothing. Sorry. Nothing."

*I hadn't brought up the party since it happened, when Summer
had her first kiss but wouldn't tell me about it. Even though I wanted
to know everything. I cursed myself for talking about it now.*

"Whatever. It's fine. We'll stay here," she said.

For the rest of lunch, we talked about our teachers and Spread
Your Wings *and Summer's spring cross-country practices. We had
gym together after lunch that day. I turned toward the hall we
always took, but Summer kept going straight.*

*"Gym is this way, silly," I said, pointing down the hall. Long
posters lined the walls with cheesy sayings. One with a picture of
a walrus in glasses asked:* Are you ready to make a big splash?

*"My allergies are acting up. I'm going to get my medicine
from the nurse," Summer said. Summer had serious enough
pollen allergies to make breathing impossible. Her eyes would
turn glassy and red like she'd been crying for hours.*

"I'll go with you." I bumped into people's backpacks trying to follow her.

"That's okay, I can go by myself."

"But we have gym. It makes sense to stay together."

"Elena, come on, I'll be right there." The words tumbled out of her mouth, but my brain replayed them in slow motion.

Elena. Come. On. I stopped short in the middle of the hall and a kid from my art class with sandy hair and green braces crashed into me. He muttered something to his friend and they both laughed. When I looked toward Summer again, she wasn't there.

A black cloud formed above my head while I walked to the gym alone. I slunk through the door of the locker room. The smell of bleach and sweat was overpowering. There was a narrow hall ahead, and to my right was a line of bathroom stalls and sinks. I kept walking until I saw the rows of lockers with the benches set up between them. The fluorescent lights above were so bright, not a single shadow to hide in and change. I thought of the shorts and T-shirt in my backpack, three sizes bigger than my sixth-grade gym clothes, thanks to my growth spurt in all the wrong places. Mom said it was normal. Maybe it was, but that didn't mean I had to reveal the new curves to everyone.

I turned on my heel into the shower stall. It was dark and concealed by a plastic curtain. I was starting to tug my dress off when I heard footsteps on the other side of the curtain, and Kendra's icy voice.

"You know you could sit with us if you want," she said. "Joey still thinks you're cute. He was bummed you never talked to him *after the party." There was shuffling as she and whoever she was with dropped their bags to the floor.*

"Elena likes our table."

Summer's voice.

"She's really attached to your hip, huh?" Sara chimed in.

A blush consumed my face, the humiliation hotter than it had ever been before.

"We're best friends."

"But don't you wish she'd leave you alone just a little bit? Don't you think she's kind of annoying?" Kendra didn't sound like she was asking a question. It was like she already knew the answer.

Summer cleared her throat.

"Yeah, I wish she'd back off."

The cloud above my head cracked open, pouring down on me until I was soaked through. I stared at the wall tiles until they blurred, until the locker room emptied out and I couldn't feel the rain anymore.

Ms. Debra had already started talking about dodgeball safety when I came out of the locker room, arms wrapped around my middle. I stood at the edge of the group where I was near Summer but not too close. Not annoyingly close. She turned her head and smiled at me. I smiled back but kept my eyes cool so she wouldn't see the hurt in my heart. I decided then that Summer could never know how much I needed her. I'd do whatever it took for those words she'd said to disappear.

Chapter
Ten

The Decision

My voice was picking up volume, singing those words about Summer, when the door opened. I slammed the notebook shut, letting it drop back into the duffel bag. Cailin walked in with a towel slung over her arm.

"Forgot my phone," she said. She crossed the room and picked her phone up off the dresser, then turned to me. "Were you just singing?"

My heart wouldn't slow down.

"Um," I said too sharply.

"Hotel walls are thin," she said. She pulled a gray scrunchie off her wrist.

"Thanks," I said, as if that made any sense.

She looked at herself in the full-length mirror on the wall, tying up her hair. I tried to watch her without being too creepy about it. I knew Cailin had to be small for her team-mates to toss her around, but in person she looked like a tiny, delicate doll. She had a squiggly scar on the side of her knee, and little pimples on her forehead. The candy-apple-colored streaks in her hair were brighter than on camera. In episode three of *On the Mat*, her team all put red in their hair to match their uniform colors. I thought back to her introduction interview on episode one.

"I'm Cailin, I'm thirteen, and I've cheered at Lone Star Elite since I was five. I've never wanted to do anything except cheer." *Her eyes flicked up to the ceiling and back down, and she squeezed the armrests on the black office chair she sat in. She was in front of a Gatorade vending machine that made her face glow blue.*

"She's only a year older than us and completely perfect," *Summer had said while we watched.*

"Completely," *I'd agreed, and later that night when I was back home, I'd opened up Cailin's page and scrolled through until my eyes hurt, studying every single picture of her eating straw-berry ice cream, or sitting on a park bench. And even though I'd done those things before too, I knew I could never make it look like she did. Like she was so happy being exactly who she was. Like her world was a place where bad things didn't happen.*

I bet Cailin had never felt a gaping empty space between her and her best friend. I shook my head and turned away before she caught me staring.

"If you're done with your call you should meet us at the

pool. If you want," Cailin said. She tugged on a piece of her bun one more time before walking out.

The Lyric Libro was at my feet, upside down on top of my clothes. I could unpack my duffel bag and pretend to be asleep when the Flyers came back. But I stared at the door instead. Past the adrenaline rush from Cailin catching me singing, and the hollow feeling of homesickness, was something sharp and hard to ignore. Summer. Watching TV on other couches, hanging out with someone else like it didn't matter that I was gone. Wishing I'd back off.

I zipped up my duffel bag and walked out of the room.

Chapter
Eleven

The Lifeguard Ring

The pool was at the end of the hall behind a wall of foggy glass. Inside the air was sticky hot and smelled like chlorine. It clung to my skin, making my black dress hug my legs tighter. I peeled the fabric away.

"You came!" Whitney announced, her smile like a warm welcome. She and Cailin and Harlow were laid out on a row of white lounge chairs. There were some teenaged girls in one-piece bathing suits on the other side of the pool, and a woman who looked like my abuelita doing laps in the water with a pink kickboard. I took the empty spot next to Whitney. There was a red-and-white-striped lifeguard ring on the wall behind us. A sign tacked underneath said, NO LIFEGUARD ON DUTY. "Did your phone call go okay?"

Summer's and Riah's whispering voices filled my head.

"It was fine," I said.

The water in the pool rippled. Even though the smell was strong, it was nice to be in the warmth, like being wrapped inside a thick blanket.

"Can we address the elephant in the room?" Harlow asked.

I clenched my jaw. Was she going to ask why I was so *quiet*? It was my least favorite question. Quiet people don't always *want* to be quiet. Sometimes the loudness inside, the voice screaming that anything we say will come out wrong or weird, just seals our mouths shut.

There's a reason people call it being painfully shy. It hurts.

The three of us looked at Harlow, waiting.

"Cailin, you're freakin' famous," she said.

Whitney whooped and I sighed with relief.

"Goodbye, elephant," Cailin said, her face shifting into a grimace. She tugged the scrunchie out of her hair, then wrapped it around her wrist and snapped the elastic against her skin.

"Do people ever call you Magnet? Like, out in the world?"

Cailin laughed under her breath.

"They call me that more than they call me Cailin. I mean, I don't know if you've noticed, or even watched the show or whatever, but my coaches and team didn't call me Cailin either. They called me Magnet until they . . . couldn't anymore. I guess."

"I watched. It was amazing," Whitney said.

In episode one, when they were interviewing Cailin in

the back room of her gym, she explained they called her
Magnet because she had never fallen out of a stunt during
a competition. It was like she stuck to the air. Magnetized.

The jets on the hot tub kicked in with a loud hum and
made us jump. Harlow shifted to her right so her whole body
was facing us.

"You probably have so many things you could be doing
now that the show's a hit," she said. The humidity in the
room was frizzing her hair. "Why'd you want to be a Flyer?"

Cailin lowered the lounge chair to the flattest position
and closed her eyes.

"You ask a lot of questions," she mumbled.

The hot tub gurgled. Harlow blinked.

"I want to be a journalist," she murmured. She tucked
the pencil farther behind her ear, the sharp lines of her face
softening. "I just got in the zone. Sorry."

Cailin exhaled through her nose.

"It's all right. I'm here because I saw the ad and it mentioned liking photography. And I really like photography."

"The pictures on your profile *are* always amazing,"
Whitney added.

I imagined her profile, all the pictures like a glimpse into
Cailin's perfect life. She opened her eyes and rolled them
back, like she was trying to stare at the striped lifeguard ring
on the wall.

"Sure. But I don't take most of those pictures."

The sound of running footsteps overtook the bubbling jets. Two boys a little older than Edgar ran into the room in identical green swim trunks, with shark fin floaties around their arms. A woman with hair the same brown as theirs rushed in behind them.

"Slow down," she called out, but they didn't. They jumped into the shallow end near where we were sitting. Water lapped up against the edge and spilled onto the tile. The boys bobbed back up, the floaties not letting them fall too far under the surface.

"Should we head back?" Whitney suggested. "I have a younger brother and if that's taught me anything it's that chaos is about to ensue."

"I have a younger brother too. Edgar," I blurted, the first words I'd said since getting to the pool. It was small, but it was something, and it was safe.

"Cool." Whitney smiled. "Don't you have a brother too, Harlow?"

Harlow snorted and rolled her eyes.

"Allegedly."

It seemed like a fact that could only be true or false, plus Harlow had blamed her brother for being late to the Tappiston. I wondered why she seemed so angry about him. The four of us peeled off our chairs. We were headed for the door when Cailin veered toward the lifeguard ring she had stared at earlier on the wall. She took out her phone and held it near the tip of the ring, then lower near the NO LIFEGUARD sign, and then up close to where a block of red and white met.

When Cailin did fall out of her stunt at the world championships, her coach gathered them all into a huddle behind the stage. The lights were dark and her teammates breathed hard. The camera found Cailin, her painted red lips pressed together, thick makeup gleaming on her face. Ponytail disheveled.

"Everyone falls, Cailin," her coach said. One of the boys on her team put a hand on Cailin's shoulder.

"I guess she's not Magnet anymore," Summer said while we watched. She had her head tipped into her hand.

"I guess not."

The hallway outside was like stepping into a freezer after being in all that heat. I smoothed my hair down and let the air cool my face. Cailin walked the closest to me at the back of the line. She was looking at the picture of the lifeguard ring she'd taken. No one was talking. I could fill in this hole in the conversation, let them see how excited I was to be a Flyer. That I was chosen for a reason even if I didn't know what it was. I could tell them how I was number one in my class, how I couldn't read a poem in language arts but wrote song lyrics in my notebook, how I had a best friend named Summer who felt so far away.

"I really liked your show, Cailin," I said.

Cailin turned and half smiled over her shoulder.

"Thanks."

Chapter Twelve

The Nail Polish

We had breakfast in the Tappiston Café at seven o'clock the next morning. It was Monday, and the early wake-up call reminded me of getting up for school. My eyes were heavy and my stomach turned. It had been hard to sleep through the city noise. Nights at home were quiet, just the hum of the streetlight, the chirping crickets. If anyone else had a hard time sleeping, they didn't show it. Whitney was still as a rock in the bed all night. And Cailin didn't do any cheer moves in her sleep, but she did snore.

Mindy sat at the head of our table while we ate. She wore a white shirt with red and green lightsabers that made an X across her chest, and black wide-leg pants. Her packet of paper was on the table next to her plate of scrambled eggs, opened up to the itinerary for the day. We each had a copy

waiting for us on the table when we came down to breakfast, and Mindy said we'd get a new one each morning. The
words were written in cursive and a thin purple ribbon was
stapled in the corner, tied into a tiny bow. I scanned it while
I drowned my pancakes in syrup. Every minute was assigned
to an activity. I took a picture of the itinerary and sent it to
Summer, wondering what she'd fill her day with. Or who.

Whitney bowed her head over her waffle, folding her
hands on the emerald-green placemat.

"My family and I always say grace. I figure that should
apply in New York, too," she said when she lifted her head
and caught me staring. My cheeks flushed and I speared a
piece of pancake to give my hands something to do. Abuelita
led my family's predinner prayer every Christmas, and my
heart would twinge with thankfulness for all the people
around me. I wondered if Whitney felt that way about being
here.

"After this we'll take the subway to Lot Eighty-Eight for
your photo shoot. Prepare to bust out your Disney princess
smiles."

Harlow choked on her eggs. I stared down at my plate,
the corners of my mouth twitching.

"Kidding." Mindy took her plate to the dirty dish bin by
the garbage cans.

Cailin groaned at her phone and rolled her eyes, typing hard on the screen. She pushed her bowl of strawberry

ge on my phone. I looked for the picture she'd taken of
e lifeguard ring, but it wasn't there. The last thing she'd
sted was a picture in baggage claim at the airport, her
ow leaned against her suitcase, the caption reading *Big
ple, Meet Cailin.* There were 347 comments underneath.
ou were my favorite on the show." "Have fun on your trip!!"
ou're not even that pretty."

The last one made me suck in my breath and turn toward
ailin, a lump in the other bed. I had always thought of her
 a fictional character from a different universe. But she
asn't. She wore cartoon character pajama pants. She snored.
Vhoever left that comment didn't even know those things.

"Do they, like, pay you for that?" Whitney asked. She had
inny gold bangles on her arm. When she dug a fork into
er waffle, they clanged together. Her short-sleeved cardigan
vas somewhat sheer and her white tank top showed under-
eath. She'd changed her outfit three times that morning.
he'd study every angle of herself in the mirror, lip between
er teeth, then disappear into the bathroom and emerge in
omething else. I hadn't said what I wanted to—that every
utfit she tried on looked perfect. I'd been the last to get
lressed, and I'd slipped my Lyric Libro into the dress I
icked for the day and sat on the edge of the bathtub to get
 song out of my head.

I never learned how to change,
Be a moon to a new phase,

yogurt to the side before holding her phone toward
across the table.

"Can you please take a picture of me?" She sh
phone a little when I didn't grab it right away. I he
watched her come into focus on the little square.
was turned on that made her look soft and sparkly.
was in a fairy wonderland and not a hotel café with
batter dispenser. She held up her hands at chest lev
facing in, and smiled without showing her teeth. I
picture and handed her phone back.

"Thanks," she mumbled.

"Sure." My mind swirled. *I just touched Cailin*
phone. I just took a picture on Cailin Carter's phone.

"What's that for?" Harlow asked. She had her
tied in two low, twisty ponytails and the pencil stil
behind her ear. Her overalls swallowed up her sm
The T-shirt she wore underneath said *New York G*
some of the letters were hidden by denim. I looked
my plate, trying not to think about how my cloth
times squeezed too tight. I raked my fork through
of maple syrup.

"Sunny Days Gel Polish, the longest-lasting po
ever wear!" Cailin said the slogan in a voice like
pinching her nose. She lifted her hands again and t
noticed her nails were painted lavender.

Last night, when I couldn't sleep, I opened u

A book to a new page.

I'm always the same.

That had been as far as I'd gotten before Whitney knocked on the door, saying she needed to switch shirts again.

"Yeah. It all goes straight to my college fund. Which is why if I don't get a picture posted for them today, my mom will lose it," Cailin answered.

I pictured her mom from the few scenes *On the Mat* showed of Cailin at home, in her kitchen, the two of them talking about how practice had gone. She looked like Cailin but stretched out, with long arms and a long chin. She chopped green peppers with a full face of makeup on. Their kitchen was painted gray, the dining table a small square just big enough for the two of them.

"That's amazing," Whitney said.

Cailin shrugged.

"Yeah, it's something. Would be better if Sunny Days Gel Polish actually lasted. But look at that." She held up her pinkie. The top corner had chipped off. "Five seconds later."

Harlow took the pencil from behind her ear and pointed it at Cailin. The rest of her body tensed up like she was fighting something.

"So it's kind of like you're lying?"

Cailin squinted and dropped her hand back to the table. I felt the tension grow like a force field between the four of us, strong enough to fill the whole café. I hoped for Mindy to come back and rush us out of here, but she was still in the line to dispose of her dirty dishes.

"That seems harsh," Whitney said. She spun the bracelets on her wrist.

"Harsh or true?" Harlow pressed the tip of her pencil into the paper napkin on the table. I spotted something like hurt in her eyes, shiny storm clouds staring down.

"It's not my fault if the stuff doesn't work. It's up to other people to decide what they want to buy." Cailin crossed her arms. I thought about the comments under her picture, how people could say such mean things when they were only seeing pieces of her. I thought about her two-person kitchen table.

"What if journalists had that mindset? Oh, I'm just going to put this out there, who cares if it's fake, people can figure out the truth for themselves." Harlow's voice turned hard and sarcastic and it made me flinch. Whitney looked over at me with her mouth in a straight, worried line.

"I'm not a journalist," Cailin said.

"You're a public figure, Magnet."

"Don't call me that!" Cailin snapped.

Harlow balled up her pencil-streaked napkin.

"Sorry. That was . . . I'm sorry. Lying just really gets to me."

She stayed quiet until Mindy came back to the table, shredding the wrinkled napkin into thin pieces and arranging them into a house shape on the table. Mindy handed each of us a paper card that said *MetroCard*. None of us looked at each other. I watched Cailin hold her card between her purple-painted fingers, and all I could think about was the bottle of Sunny Days Gel Polish on my dresser at home, the one Summer and I split the cost of last month. Because Cailin Carter told us it would last forever.

The Disney Adult

The subway ride to the photo shoot was bumpy and quiet. It was stuffy inside the car, and it smelled like the recycling center where Mom and I deposited cans. We found seats in one long row. I sat next to Mindy at the end. A map was posted to the wall, crisscrossed with blue and red and yellow lines. I remembered we took the red one to get to Times Square in December. There weren't enough empty seats on the subway that day, so Summer and I had to stand. We'd let go of the metal pole and tried to balance while the ground shook under our feet.

I pulled out my phone to text her now.

On the subway. Remember when we both fell on our butts because we weren't holding on?

I tried not to notice that she hadn't responded to the

picture of the itinerary. She was probably on a run. It wasn't because she'd decided not to be happy for me about being a Flyer. It wasn't because we'd been drifting further apart, maybe since Joey Demarco's Halloween party. Or that since I was in New York and not right next door, it wasn't because I'd been replaced.

"Do you live in the city, Mindy?" Harlow asked. She leaned forward in her seat.

"Sure do," Mindy answered. "In the smallest studio apartment you've ever seen. *With* a roommate. And two cats. But it's walking distance to my graduate classes at NYU."

"Are you in school for journalism?"

Mindy shook her head. "Negative."

"So then what do you want to be when you . . ." Harlow stopped herself. Mindy smiled and stood from her seat, then turned to face us. She gripped the metal pole.

"When I grow up," she finished the question. The light-sabers on her shirt looked like the lines on the subway map.

"I worded it the wrong way. You're clearly grown up," Harlow explained.

Mindy tilted her head, her orange hair falling to the side.

"Really? I sure hope not," she said.

Cailin and Whitney and I watched while Harlow and Mindy went back and forth with their questions and answers. I thought about how it was a therapist's job to do that—to ask the right questions to lead someone to their breakthrough.

Harlow made it look so easy. She didn't stammer or blush until her whole face was red. The subway squealed to a stop a few times. A muffled announcer told passengers to mind the gap between the car and the platform.

"Have you all ever heard of Disney adults?" Mindy asked.

I shook my head and saw the rest of the Flyers do the same.

"They're people my age or older who go to Disney by themselves, or with friends, but we're not pushing strollers around. We're not there with our families. We're twenty-five-year-olds in sequined mouse ears and character T-shirts, getting our picture taken with the Little Mermaid. And people think we don't belong there!"

My eyes shifted over to Cailin. I wondered what she thought of when Mindy mentioned Disney World; that's where the world championships had been. Where an arena full of people had sucked in their breath when she fell. One giant, loud gasp. She stared down at her phone, her face not giving away what she was feeling, the dark tunnel zipping by in the window behind her.

"But what I would like to know is when does someone become too old for magic?" Mindy continued. "I don't feel like an adult. I don't think I ever will. And I don't want to. Even when I have a house or a partner or grandkids."

"Like a partner in crime?" Harlow asked.

Mindy's feet shuffled a little when the subway heaved to another stop.

"More like a partner in life. A wife. Or a husband. Whoever they are, I hope they're wearing those ears and eating Dole Whips right next to me forever."

A wife or *a husband?*

I let those words roll around in my head. It sounded nice, Mindy and whoever she chose to love walking around the Magic Kingdom with tall swirls of pineapple and ice cream.

Mindy cleared her throat.

"To answer your original question, Harlow, I don't want to be just one thing. I want to be all the things."

Harlow nodded, and I felt like I'd just witnessed an interview that had gotten off track, but I felt like I knew more about Mindy now, which I guess is what interviews are supposed to do.

The subway stopped and Mindy told us this was where we needed to get off. This station was outside, not underground, and it was warm when we stepped onto the platform and down a long flight of stairs. The streets here were small and sunlit. I'd never seen New York like this before, without the giant billboards and neon lights and swarms of people. Here things felt cozier. Like even though it was still a big city, there was a place where things slowed down. Mindy said we were in Astoria, Queens.

"Studio's up ahead! Second star to the right and straight on till morning," Mindy shouted. She swung both her arms out to the side like she might take flight with Peter Pan. "Ha! Kidding."

A smile spread across my face. I snuck glances at Whitney, Harlow, and Cailin, and they were smiling too.

"It does kind of feel like we're going to Neverland," Whitney said. The gold headband in her hair matched her bracelets, and all of it sparkled.

The four of us laughed, and what happened at breakfast seemed to float away.

Chapter
Fourteen

The Microphone

We stopped in front of a building with LOT 88 spelled out in shiny brass letters above the entrance. Scaffolding covered the studio. I watched Cailin snap a picture of the construction as we walked through.

The inside reminded me of a warehouse. The floor was cement and the walls showed their skeletons, all beams and bolts. A white backdrop hung down from a frame to the right where three cameras sat on tripods. Props were set up on a table—a beach ball, a teal guitar, a giant spatula. My eyes fell on the racks of clothes in the middle of the room.

"Welcome to the studio. The greats have all been shot here, so consider yourself one of them, and I'm not kidding," Mindy said. She stepped over to the prop table and picked up the beach ball, then batted it toward us. "Your bio photo shoot is all about letting the readers know who you are through the lens of the camera. We have clothes and accessories for you to use, and Whitney, since we know how interested you are in fashion, we're going to let you style everyone."

Whitney's bracelets slid up and down when she covered her mouth and jumped. When she landed, her glasses were crooked and her curls were slightly askew.

The outfits were organized by size and color. I sifted through the blue section in large, past knit cardigans and jumpsuits. I tried not to notice everyone else searching through the smaller sizes.

"What's your style, Harlow?" Whitney asked.

Harlow tilted her head.

"I'd say a laid-back reporter but with a sporty flair," she answered, motioning toward her denim and T-shirt combo. "Resporty!"

Whitney laughed and pulled a red plaid flannel from the rack. "White tank underneath. And some jeans. Dark wash and ripped." She handed Harlow the shirt. Harlow slung it over her shoulder and looked through the folded ripped jeans. I shifted my gaze away from the pile.

In March, Summer and I took old pairs of jeans and cut them up with scissors, since the already-ripped pairs at the mall were so expensive. She'd taken the cheese grater from her house, and we sat on my bedroom floor destroying the denim.

When we were done, we put our pairs on, Summer changing

in my room and me slipping into the bathroom. I stood in front of the full-length mirror on the back of the door and stared at the holes, at my skin popping through. I tore the jeans off. They didn't look the same on me as on the models in the store windows, or the other girls in my grade. And when I walked back into my room with the jeans draped over my arm, I noticed they didn't look like they did on Summer, either. She did lunges by the Flyers wall, testing out the stretchiness of the fabric. She asked why I'd taken them off and I said I didn't want to bother, since Mom would never let me wear ripped jeans anyway.

"What about you, Elena?" Whitney's voice snapped me out of the memory.

I sifted through the rack, wishing I could just grab a dress and be good to go.

"I wear a lot of dresses," I said.

"Try this." Whitney handed me a bubblegum-pink sundress. I took it and went to the dressing room area set up behind a white wall in the back of the studio.

Fairy lights twined across the top of the dressing room mirror. There was a rack on the wall and a bench to sit on. I folded up the floral dress I was wearing and left it on the bench, then changed into the dress Whitney had chosen for me. The skirt was the kind that would fan out if I spun around; the material was soft on my skin. *Diagnosis: feeling bad about your body. Treatment: this dress.*

I stepped out. The curtain blocking the next dressing

room slid open at the same time. Whitney came out in a
gray shirt and striped shorts with a big bow in the front. She
wore sandals with ribbon that tied around her shins.

"That looks perfect on you," she said.

"Thanks for picking it out," I answered, my cheeks
matching the color of the dress. Whitney darted to the mir-
rors at the end of the line of dressing rooms and ran a hand
over her hair.

"Ouch!" she yelped.

I rushed over.

"What happened?" I asked.

"My hair is caught in the shirt zipper." She yanked on a
curl. "Ouch!"

"Let me help."

I found the zipper under her hair and started easing the
strands out in small sections.

"I've been meaning to ask you something," Whitney said.
I kept my fingers moving.

"Okay."

"I probably don't even need to—you seem so quiet and
trustworthy and everything—but can you not tell anyone
about what happened at the train station? Like, when you
first found me."

I thought about Whitney's breath coming out too hard
and the look in her eyes. The constellations on Grand
Central's ceiling.

"I won't say anything," I promised, trying to ignore that she'd called me *quiet*.

"It's just I haven't told anyone about how that happens to me—" she started.

I caught Whitney's eye in the mirror. The lights glared against the lenses of her glasses.

"Not even your parents?"

"No." Her voice was soft but serious. I pulled the last piece of hair from the sharp part of the zipper. "Whenever my family and I say our prayers, my parents add how much we have to be thankful for. Our house, our health, each other. Like, how can I tell them how anxious I feel when they don't think there's anything to be anxious about? Nothing I can point to and say, 'Yeah, that's what's bothering me.'"

Her questions reminded me of the adults in my life telling me to speak up, saying it wasn't as hard as I was making it out to be.

"I understand," I said.

Whitney opened her mouth to say something but Cailin walked over, wearing a black tank top and red corduroy skirt that matched the highlights in her hair.

"Mindy said it's time to start. Well, actually she said, 'Get them out here or I'll be a Flyer, ha, kidding,' but you get it," she said with a smirk.

"Coming!" Harlow stepped out of the dressing room

closest to the mirror, directly next to where Whitney and I stood. Whitney's eyes went wide.

"I didn't know you were in there," she said.

"I'm stealthy. All good journalists are." Harlow looked at Whitney like she was apologizing. The flannel shirt was rolled up to her elbows. She walked out of the dressing room area with Cailin. I stared at the flimsy fabric that had separated Harlow from my conversation with Whitney, remembering how easy it had been to hear Summer talk about me through a curtain just like that one.

Whitney took a shaky breath. Before I could think about it, I reached out and grabbed her hand.

"It's going to be okay," I said.

I wished there had been someone to say that to me in the locker room. Maybe that's why it came out of my mouth without me trying to stop myself. I wanted to be that person for someone else so badly it overrode the fear. Whitney smiled and nodded, squeezing my hand once before she let go.

"You're right." She shook her shoulders. "I'm just going to switch shirts. I'll be right out."

She disappeared into a dressing room. Outside, the photo shoot had started. Three photographers stood behind the cameras dressed in all black. Cailin was on the white tarp with her arms crossed while Mindy tried to hand her a pair of pom-poms.

"We figured you'd want to show your love of cheerleading," Mindy explained. She raised the pom-poms in the air. "Go team."

Cailin curled her hands into fists.

"I'm an all-star cheerleader. We don't use pom-poms. And we don't say 'go team.' We are the team." She stalked over to the prop table and ran her hands over the electric keyboard, the paintbrushes, the chef's hat and mixing bowl. She stopped at a turquoise Polaroid camera and picked it up. "I want to use the camera."

Mindy made eye contact with the photographer, and then looked back at Cailin.

"You're sure you don't want to highlight your time on *On the Mat*?"

Cailin stood on the white tarp again with the camera in her hands. She looked shrunken in. Defeated. So tiny she might just disappear.

"I'm here because I like photography and want to learn more about it. Not because I was on a show. Right?" There was a fire in her eyes.

Mindy said nothing for a second too long.

"Of course not." Mindy pulled the packet of paper out from under her lightsaber shirt. "We're actually going to let you set up the shots for everyone else. How's that?"

The lights shone on Cailin's face and reminded me of her Miami picture, her head leaning up to the sun. But even though she looked the same, had the same pointed nose and red streaks in her hair, the Cailin on the tarp didn't seem like the posed, glowing girl on the towel. She lifted the Polaroid camera and started to pretend to take pictures, crouching and bending like she was capturing different angles, like she did with the lifeguard ring at the pool.

When it was Harlow's turn, Cailin and the assistants set up a black stool and tiny table with an old-fashioned typewriter on top. Harlow kept the pencil behind her ear while she pretended to type, smiling down at the keys. For Whitney they brought out a headless beige mannequin. She wrapped a tape measure around its middle and pressed pins into its fabric skin.

My heart pounded while I watched them, so smiley and confident doing the things they loved. The things that would help the readers get to know them. I ran my eyes across the prop table. There were no parts-of-a-cell worksheets. There were no pebbles to toss from a window. There was no Summer.

"Your turn, Elena," the photographer said. He adjusted some settings on his camera and gave me a thumbs-up. Cailin waited on the tarp.

"What are you thinking?" Cailin asked. With Harlow and Whitney she didn't even have to ask.

"I guess the books?" I pointed to the stack at the end of the table. "I like school."

Cailin followed my eyes to the table and tapped her chin. More polish had peeled off her nails.

"Hold that thought."

She came back with a microphone, silver with sparkles on the handle. It was heavy and unfamiliar in my hand. My skin jolted when I grabbed it, like the handle was electric. I pictured my Lyric Libro flying open in front of everyone, all my thoughts and songs on display.

"No, I can't."

"I know I caught you singing the other day. And I couldn't hear you all that well, but I did see how you looked. You looked like my teammates do before we perform. I swear."

Cailin walked away with the wire to the microphone in her hand, guiding it so it would lie across the tarp. I stared down at the little holes in the top of the microphone and wished one would suck me in.

"Okay, go ahead and start," the lead photographer said. The other three Flyers sat in folding chairs behind him.

I lifted the microphone to my mouth and tried to smile like all the other Flyers I'd seen in my copies of the magazine. The microphone cord dragged on the ground like a ball and chain when I moved around. I couldn't focus on the camera. My brain was full of jumbled up lyrics.

"Doing great, Elena," the photographer said, but the tone of his voice and lowered camera made it clear that I wasn't.

"I can keep trying," I said. The studio's sound system

played one of my favorites from the radio, where the background music stopped and it was just the singer's voice belting out the lyrics.

"It might help if you actually sing," Cailin shouted with a smile.

The photographer picked up the camera again. "She's right. Even when artists are lip-synching, it helps them to actually sing."

The idea made me want to run back down the street, back to the subway with its crisscrossed map on the wall, back home. But the microphone cord was a tether keeping me there. Cailin, Harlow, and Whitney nodded at me, encouraging smiles on their faces. I had to try.

I picked the microphone up again and the camera flashed. It left purple spots in my vision, blocked everything else out. I tuned in to the lyrics coming from the speaker and started to sing in my soft and shaky voice. I didn't pay attention to who was in the room. It was just me and the music.

I didn't stop until the final note of the song had played. I came back down to earth where the Flyers were standing behind the camera, clapping.

Chapter Fifteen

The Headquarters

After we wrapped up at Lot 88, we took the subway into Midtown Manhattan. It was busier when we got off, the New York I remembered from our holiday trip. I saw the coffee shop our parents had ducked into for cappuccinos, the souvenir store where I bought Summer a snow globe for Hanukkah. Food trucks were up against the curb selling hot dogs and fries, and it all smelled like summertime.

Mindy brought us into the lobby of the tallest building I'd ever actually been in.

"Is this the *Spread Your Wings* headquarters?" Harlow asked. Her eyes glinted like the shiny tip of a pen.

"Technically, this is a lobby," Mindy answered, and winked. She shrugged her You've Got a Friend in Me bag up higher on her shoulder. "But yes, we're going up to the office."

We were quiet on the elevator ride to the twentieth floor, like we were all too full of anticipation to say anything. The elevator music swelled with violins and got to the biggest, most dramatic part when the doors opened up again.

A patch of purple carpet led up to the floor-to-ceiling doors, the *Spread Your Wings* logo printed on the frosted glass. I wanted to run my fingers over the letters just to be sure this was all real. Was I really walking through the maze of hallways, seeing the cover of every issue on the wall in a purple frame? There were cubicles on the left with dividers between them. *Spread Your Wings* employees typed at computers at small, snow-white desks, some of them decorated with pictures and stickers and cactuses in clay pots. It all had a quiet, soothing hum to it, like the inside of a library.

"This is some of our writing team," Mindy said, motioning to the cubicles.

"How do you get a job like this?" Harlow asked. Her eyes wandered everywhere. "In a place like this?"

A writer with a shaved head and pink lipstick smiled and waved at me. She had superhero stickers on her computer monitor.

"Luck," Mindy answered.

Harlow's forehead creased. She fiddled with the pencil behind her ear.

Mindy led us to a room labeled CONFERENCE 1205B. A long table with cushy-looking black chairs ran down the middle. Each seat had a pad of lined paper and a purple pen. The walls were painted violet with white stars, and a dry-erase board hung on the far wall with the words *Personal Essay* written inside a cloud shape. I stepped closer to the table and saw small ivory cards with our names written in purple script. I was next to Harlow on one side, and Whitney and Cailin were on the other. I took a picture of the setup—the pen and the paper and the stars on the wall—and sent it to Summer. The four unanswered texts I'd sent her filled up the screen and made my heart skip a beat.

I heard footsteps from the hallway outside and a woman walked in, the most glamorous person I'd ever seen in real life. Her hair was black and parted right down the middle, and it was so long it touched her hips. The flowy shirt she wore was bright white against her brown skin. It was the kind of shirt other people would be afraid to wear in case they spilled something on it, but she held a steaming purple mug in her hand like there was no way a stain would happen on her watch. I recognized her from the Letter from the Editor section at the beginning of every issue. In April she'd written, *Remember, dear reader, that your heart is everything,* and I'd cut out the words and taped them to my wall.

"Flyers, meet Akshita Balay, the lead editor at *Spread Your Wings*," Mindy said with so much enthusiasm I felt like we should stand and applaud.

"Welcome," Akshita said. She placed her mug on the

table and sat down. The string from a tea bag hung over the edge. Now that she was closer, I could smell the tea, citrus mixed with cinnamon. "Meeting the Flyers is truly my favorite part of the job, so I want to congratulate all of you, and thank you for being here. There would be no September issue, *the* back-to-school issue, without the content you help build."

She paused for a second, looking at each one of us, her eyes deep and shimmering. The urgency in them made me sit up straighter. She was telling us we were important and I believed her. In that moment I believed that I was supposed to be here.

"I feel like school just ended. It's strange to think about going back already," Whitney said.

Akshita smiled and took a sip of her tea.

"One of the many interesting elements of magazine production. We are always thinking ahead. We live in the future."

In the seat next to me I saw Harlow start a bulleted list on her notepad. *Live in the future,* she wrote. She used her pencil instead of the purple pen. Mindy came around with red juice in tall, thin glasses and put one in front of each of us.

"As you may know, each of you will be contributing an essay for the issue. This essay can be about anything important to you. We want you to dig deep, tap into your creative wells, and let our readers—your readers—get to know you. We hope your experiences with us will also provide some inspiration."

Harlow added *Dig deep. Creative well. Inspiration.* When Akshita stood to face the whiteboard, her back to us, I saw Cailin turn in her chair toward the wall, lift her phone, and aim it at a cluster of stars. Her finger pressed into the side button to take a picture.

"We'll be going over the components of a compelling personal essay, but first we're going to start with some brainstorming." Akshita ran her hand across the silver bar under the board. "Oh. No marker."

"I'll get one!" Mindy declared, and waved her arms, knocking over a glass of the punch. It clattered against the table but didn't break, pouring red liquid over the lightsabers printed on her chest. She stared down. "Holy Hercules, that did not just happen."

I heard Harlow make a muffled laughing sound in her throat. Whitney and Cailin rushed to cover their mouths. I had to look away, my heart aching for her. I was always fumbling my words the way Mindy had fumbled that glass. *Diagnosis: an embarrassing moment. Treatment: try your best to brush past it. In Mindy's case, find some extra-strength stain remover.*

"It's okay, Mindy. Go . . . clean off," Akshita said.

Mindy hurried out of the conference room, arms crossed over her chest, orange hair hiding her face. Akshita sat back down. She took a long sip of her tea.

"Another favorite part of *Spread Your Wings*. The unexpected," she said when she set the mug back down. She smiled and her teeth were as white and straight as a picket fence. "But what you can expect is exploring this great city. Working with our writers and photographers. And developing your essays, which we consider human interest writing."

Harlow frowned.

"So we won't be doing much investigating? Into the hard-hitting news?"

Akshita dipped the tea bag up and down, the sound like raindrops hitting a puddle.

"Our stories are an investigation of the heart. What could be more hard-hitting than that?"

Harlow stared down at the notepad. She wrote *investigation of the heart* between the lines.

Akshita told us to do some free writing to get down some ideas for our essays. She said free writing was how we would unlock the treasure trunks in our heads. I thought about what my trunk would be filled with. My Lyric Libro would sit next to the stack of movies my family watches on Thursdays. There would be a film reel of memories of Summer and me sitting on the boat launch, planning where we'd sail off to.

"We should sail to Puerto Rico. I've never been but I have family there. We can stay with them," I offered one day last summer. The day was humid and foggy and my skin was sticky from the heat.

"That's not the point. We're sailing to places where no one

knows us," Summer said, kicking her legs. Her feet were bare,
her sneakers tipped over next to her thigh. They didn't have my
signature on them yet.

"Why don't we want anyone to know us?" I asked.

She sniffed.

"You can be anyone you want if no one knows you."

I watched the sun glare against the water. It was too bright
to see far into the distance.

"Antarctica, then?" I asked. "We can live with the penguins."

Summer laughed and reached down, splashing some lake
water at my ankles.

"Yeah. Antarctica."

I didn't want to write about that piece of treasure, so I
just wrote *free write*. Mindy walked back in. She had put on
a loose blue sweatshirt with the *Spread Your Wings* logo. The
soiled shirt was folded up in her hand. She placed a dry-erase
marker on the table next to Akshita, then sat back in her seat,
tucking the shirt into her bag.

I skipped down a few spaces and in smaller letters started
a song.

A stain spreads out; it grows and grows.

Whether it'll come out no one knows.

Some stains set, some stains heal.

But that doesn't change the way stains feel.

"You have amazing handwriting," Cailin said.

I slammed my hand over the page hard enough to make

everyone jump, to make Akshita drop her tea bag into her mug.

"Oh. Thanks." Heat shot up the back of my neck.

"No problem," Cailin said slowly.

I waited for everyone to look away, for the blush to leave my face, then wrote a big *X* through the lyrics. I didn't write anything else. The treasure trunk in my head was bolted shut, so I unlocked my phone instead. Summer still hadn't answered.

The Donut Hole

James was one of the three *Spread Your Wings* staff photographers we had met that morning, and Akshita told us he'd be tagging along for the rest of our activities. He wore a black baseball cap and said things like "work it" and "that's the stuff," which reminded me of Dad when he tried to be funny. Mom would laugh so hard she'd snort, and that would make all of us laugh all over again. My heart squeezed thinking about them, thinking about being where everything was familiar. I let the rest of the group get farther ahead of me and dialed my home number.

"It's Elena," Dad exclaimed when he answered. "Everyone, it's Elena. She didn't forget about us when she became famous."

I smiled and pressed the phone into my cheek like that

would bring me closer to them. The sound of Mom's footsteps came through the receiver, followed by Edgar's singing clownfish.

"Put her on speaker," she said. "Tell us everything."

A taxi honked its horn and I startled. The crossing sign on the other side of the street showed an orange hand. *Stop.* The rest of the Flyers were on the other side. Whitney turned and waved me over.

"Lenny? Are you all right?" Dad asked, his voice serious.

I felt split in half, one ear full of home and the other full of the sounds of the city. They clashed like I couldn't be in both places at once.

"I'll call you back," I said. I put my phone in my pocket and hustled the rest of the way across the street, feeling farther from home and my family and Summer than I had since I'd arrived in New York. Whitney turned back again to smile at me, and the afternoon light was bright, and it didn't feel so bad to be exactly where I was. The sun still shone when I was on my own.

We stopped at a gourmet donut shop called the Donut Hole two blocks away from the *Spread Your Wings* building. The name was painted on the window, and the *O*s were pink-frosted donuts. I knew it was a Flyers tradition to stop at the Donut Hole. Every September issue had a two-page spread of pictures of the Flyers with their hands wrapped around decorated donuts.

"Why do all the Flyers come here?" Harlow asked.

"Donuts are Akshita's favorite," James answered, then snapped a picture of me peering through a donut *O* to see the real donuts inside. "Fierce."

When we were all inside, Mindy stayed at the door.

"I'm going to the gift shop next door for a new shirt before I melt in this hoodie. James, can you keep an eye on the minions?"

"You got it," he answered.

The café was almost empty and smelled like berries and chocolate syrup. We took a table by the window. I sat in one of the inside chairs and pressed my shoulder into the sun-warmed glass, allowing the afternoon rays to thaw out the air-conditioning goose bumps across my skin.

"I'll give you all some space," James said. He handed his boxy black camera to Cailin. "Want to take the shots?"

Cailin's face lit up. I'd seen that look before, on episode four of *On the Mat* when her team qualified to attend the world championships.

"Yes please," she said. She held the camera between her hands like a baby bird when she sat down, studying the lens and all the buttons.

A waiter in a sugar-dusted black apron came by our table and dropped a list in front of each of us. The flavors of donuts were typed out in swirly letters, with a checkbox next to each one. He reached into his apron for a handful of yellow golf pencils, said he'd be back in a few to get our orders, and disappeared into the kitchen. I read through the list. Mint Mayhem, Carrot Cake Chaos, Fruity Pebble Power. If Summer were here, she'd check Blueberry Bonanza.

"What are you going to write your essays about?" Whitney asked the table. She was across from me, and I could see my reflection in her glasses.

"Probably being on the show. I have a lot to say." Cailin held up the camera and took a test shot of the window, THE DONUT HOLE spelled backward.

"I would read that." Whitney checked the box for Mint Mayhem. "Harlow?"

Harlow was looking at the menu like it was in a different language. She rolled the golf pencil between her fingers.

"I don't know. I thought we'd be doing more reporting. Like on what's going on in the city. Or what's in an Everything but the Kitchen Sink donut."

"Only one way to find out," I said, and everyone laughed when Harlow checked the box. It felt warmer than the sunlight on my shoulder.

The waiter collected our checklists, then came back with a big tray of donuts on peach-colored plates. He put our orders in front of each of us. My Caramel Craze was coated in toffee crumbles and beige buttercream. I took a bite. The donut was soft and sweet with a caramel core. I noticed Cailin had ordered the Blueberry Bonanza, and fresh

blueberries were planted like flowers in the indigo frosting. We ate in silence for a second, and the I'm-a-Flyer feeling shot through me like a sugar rush, like it had when I sang at Lot 88 and when Akshita first welcomed us.

Cailin picked up the camera and aimed it at Harlow.

"Say 'Everything but the Kitchen Sink.'"

Harlow picked up the donut, covered in peanuts and pretzels and peppermint candies, and held it to her eye like a monocle. She smiled and said the words, and then leaned closer to Whitney, who picked up her donut too and did the same pose.

"Hurry, I'm getting frosting on my glasses!" Whitney warned.

Cailin smiled and I thought she looked happier than in any scene in *On the Mat*.

I took out my phone to take a picture of my donut to post to my page, even though a bite was taken out. Before I could post, a new picture from Summer's page loaded on the screen. Cailin clicked the camera to take another shot, this time with the lens on me as I stared at my phone.

There were two sets of sneakers dangling over the edge of a splintery dock. One pair that left dirt on the floor of my language arts classroom. Another with my name on the toe.

Summer and Riah at the boat launch. Summer took Riah to the boat launch.

Cailin looked at the display on the camera and then at m

"I think I caught something," she said.

I put the phone facedown on the table and tore a piece off my donut.

"It's nothing."

Harlow narrowed her eyes, studying me like a subject in one of her stories.

"Your body language says different." She pointed at my dismantled donut.

Tears sprung hot behind my eyes, making me feel mad and stupid and lonely all at once. I took a shallow breath of the chocolatey air.

"You can tell us," Whitney said.

Something about the bright-colored plates, the city outside, the Flyers leaning in closer, made me feel safe. Heat wasn't crawling into my cheeks. My throat wasn't locked tight. It was like being in Summer's sunroom—a space I thought I could trust.

"My best friend, Summer, and I have this place. The boat launch in our town. It's ours. Or, it used to be." I showed them the picture without looking at it again. I couldn't stand to see the water shining under their shoes. "She brought someone else there."

Cailin put James's camera down to look closer.

"She used Poppy. Good filter."

"I'm not sure that's Elena's point here," Whitney said. She scooped a dollop of green frosting with her pinkie. "She's lost something sacred."

"You need to be honest with her about it," Harlow said. Her voice was soft. "Send her a text."

I gulped.

"What should I say?" I asked.

"Say that you saw the picture and want to know why of all the places in your town of . . ." She waited for me to finish the sentence.

"Franklin City, Connecticut."

"Franklin City, she chose to hang out with someone else in your spot."

I opened my messages. The thought of actually sending that to Summer scared me more than the extra credit poem reading. More than telling her what I overheard her say in the locker room. I typed that was our place and let the cursor blink a few times. The send button blurred into a green blob.

"It's only scary until you do it," Cailin said. "That's what my coach says when he wants me to try new things."

I pressed send.

The little bubble that showed Summer was typing popped up right away; it jumped on the screen for a few too many seconds before her answer appeared.

She's my friend.

The answer made me madder. Made me want that dock to collapse and sink like a shipwreck. I typed without asking for advice. This time it poured out like lyrics.

Yeah, I know. But the boat launch?

Another bubble appeared. Harlow, Whitney, and Cailin watched me while I waited.

We don't have to share everything, Elena.

I stared at the screen, wondered what the camera would catch if Cailin snapped this moment where the world crashed down on me like a wave.

"What did she say?" Whitney asked. Some sugar had tipped out of the jar by the napkin dispenser, and she drew a star into the grains with her pinkie.

"All good," I answered quickly. "We're always good."

I smiled and took another bite of my donut to try to convince them that I was okay, swallowing past the lump in my throat.

Chapter Seventeen

The Party

I couldn't sleep again. Mom used to tell me that when I wouldn't sleep as a baby, she took me for walks up and down our street. Back and forth as many times as it took, no matter what color blue the sky was, until I drifted off.

The lights were out and the city shone in through the windows. Our room still smelled like the pizza we'd had delivered for dinner (half green pepper for Whitney, who was a vegetarian, and half pepperoni for us meat eaters). Whitney was curled on her side next to me, and Cailin's soft snoring came from the other bed. I swung my legs out from under the satin sheets and slid my feet into the sandals I'd left on the floor. They clip-clopped too loudly when I walked, so I rose on my tiptoes and crept across the room, past the cardboard pizza boxes and Whitney's duffel bag and Harlow's clothes, until I made it to the hallway.

I took the stairs instead of the elevator. The stairwell was a different world from the rest of the hotel. It had white cement walls and scuffed linoleum floors like the classrooms at my school, like the builders forgot to come back and make this part pretty. I veered out of the stairwell to the second floor and walked toward the pool; I knew where it was and what it would smell like and I hoped that maybe that would be comforting.

"You lost?" a voice asked from behind me. A woman with a thick brown braid and white chef's coat pushed a cart of dirty dishes.

"No, I'm just going to the pool," I answered, even though I was wearing plaid pajamas and not a bathing suit.

"Closes pretty soon. It's almost eleven."

"I know. I just want to put my feet in."

"Careful. Last girl who went in there alone right before closing time wound up drowning." She pressed the button next to the elevator.

"Is that true?" I asked, my heart giving one big beat like it was gasping for breath.

The woman shrugged. The elevator beeped and the doors opened. She pushed her cart through. I heard her laugh when the doors closed.

I pressed my back into the wall and slid down to the floor, curling my legs up into my chest. My phone was in my pocket. I opened my messages with Summer and her last one was still there, still waiting for me to reply.

We don't have to share everything, Elena.

It wasn't the first time she'd said something like that to me.

When Summer and I went to the fateful Halloween party in Joey Demarco's basement, I was a flapper and wore a fringy dress and Mom's shortest heels. Summer dressed as a gumball machine in a red shirt with colored cotton balls glued on. We huddled together in the basement, eating Skittles and whispering. It was fun to get dressed up, and to be around our classmates outside of school, even if we weren't talking to anyone but each other. The feeling was grown up and glowy all at the same time.

Kendra Blair had come up to us in our spot by the stairs and tapped on Summer's shoulder. She was dressed like a vampire with a trail of fake blood in the corner of her mouth.

"Joey wants to kiss you," she said. Her voice was garbled by plastic fangs.

Summer's eyes widened. She twisted up the Skittles wrapper in her hand.

"How do you know that?" Summer asked.

"He told me. Look, he's going outside now." Kendra pointed to the sliding door on the other end of the basement. Joey was walking out. He was dressed like a baseball player in a pinstriped uniform, and he waved before disappearing into the dark. "He wants you to meet him in the driveway."

Summer glanced at me. I opened my mouth and shrugged, words lodged in my throat, unable to escape. Kendra giggled and it sounded as evil as she looked. Her vampire outfit billowed around her like a cloud of black smoke when she walked away, toward the snack table where Sara Smith and her other friends were standing.

I felt the Skittles melting in my palm. I looked down and saw the rainbow-colored stain on my skin. "Monster Mash" played on the radio.

"Should I go?" Summer asked. She adjusted her cotton-ball shirt. I saw goose bumps on her arms.

"Do you want to?"

"I don't know. I've never . . . done that."

"There's a first time for everything."

The answer was braver than I felt. When I looked around the room, everyone's costumes seemed scarier, like the make-believe part was gone and everything was real. The vampires and ghosts. My best friend was about to have her first kiss.

"Okay. I'm going to go." Summer took a breath and crossed the basement, leaving me alone by the stairs in my flapper dress and wobbly heels.

She wasn't gone long. A few minutes later she slid the door open and walked fast back over to me, a pink cotton ball falling off her shirt to the dusty cement floor. Joey walked in right after her. He disappeared into a group of his friends, all dressed like baseball players too.

*I handed Summer another pack of Skittles from the candy
bowl nearby.*

*"Thanks," she said. She tore the package and shoved a hand-
ful in her mouth, chewing slowly.*

*"So? Did you?" I asked. My heart beat hard under my flapper
dress.*

*"Yeah," she said. She ate another Skittle, this one as green as
her eyes.*

*"And?" I realized how crazy my voice sounded, how out of
control. Summer had done something I'd never done. Something
that would make us different even though I'd always thought of
us as two halves of the same person.*

"It was fine." She shrugged.

*"That's all I get? Summer, you just crossed the kissing line! I
need to know everything."*

Summer's eyes didn't look right. They were far away and dark.

"We don't have to tell each other everything."

*All the lights and the sounds in Joey's basement faded away,
until it was just me and Summer and those words between us. I
guess we didn't have to tell each other everything; I just thought
we always would. I felt a rope wind itself around my waist, tug-
ging me away from Summer.*

"I know that," I said.

*"So let's just forget about it," Summer said, and started to
dance with her eyes closed, the empty Skittles wrapper still balled
up in her fist.*

I stared at the blinking cursor in the text box on my phone, then typed I'm sorry. I backspaced until the message disappeared. I know this year has been different, I wrote, and deleted it. My eyes filled up with every attempt at a text, none of the words feeling right. What I really wanted to say was that I was mad. Mad at Summer for not telling me about her first kiss. Mad at her for the locker room, and the bus ride to the winter field trip where Kendra and Sara made fun of me and Summer joined in. Mad at myself for letting it all happen without saying a word.

Are we even still friends?

I sat in the hall and wrote and deleted messages to Summer until I finally felt tired enough to go upstairs and close my eyes. I drifted off to the sound of rushing cars.

Chapter
Eighteen

The Team Meeting

Our itinerary on Tuesday morning said we'd spend most of the day at headquarters. All through our subway ride and our walk to the building I resisted the urge to text Summer, to send her pictures of the busy streets and that souvenir store with the snow globes. *Diagnosis: silence. Treatment: fill it up with apologies.* I wanted us to be fine. That's all I'd ever wanted, even if it meant burying the hard stuff. But right now it felt like I was in that deep hole where I'd hidden the times Summer had hurt me, and I couldn't find the way to climb out.

The office was busier than it was yesterday. Instead of sitting at cubicles, the staff was up and shuffling around with manila folders and laptops in their hands. They all seemed headed for a door farther down the hall than the conference room we'd been in yesterday.

"There are more people here," Harlow noted. The four of us stood at the entrance to the office with Mindy, watching the world move at hyper-speed.

"Everyone is in the office on Tuesdays. It's team meeting day." Mindy spread her arms and guided us down the hall until we were part of the crowd, like bees buzzing around in a hive. I felt a little like I'd been stung.

"We're part of the team," Whitney whispered in my ear. She tugged on the hem of her red silky shirt. This morning she'd asked the rest of us which jeans to wear with it, and all of us picked the cropped ones with bedazzled butterflies on the front pockets. She'd put them on and stared at the butterflies in the mirror until the second we had to leave.

We walked into a conference room with a long, wide table and extra chairs stuffed inside. There were stars on the wall like the room we'd been in yesterday, but the paint was blue instead of purple. Akshita was at the front of the room in a white suit. She waved us over to four empty chairs. The whiteboard on the wall and the murmur of conversation reminded me of stepping into a classroom, but I didn't have a textbook to hide behind.

"Everyone's so excited you're here," Akshita said when we sat down. I was closest to her at the edge of the table. Her mug steamed in front of me. "We love Flyer week."

"Do we get to be part of this meeting?" Harlow asked. She already had her notebook out.

Akshita twisted the tea bag in her mug around her pinkie. "Of course. You can participate as much as you'd like."

I thought about Mrs. Parekh's syllabus, how participation was ten percent of our final grade. I didn't want to Elena-fail at being a Flyer. Akshita cleared her throat and the room quieted down.

"Happy Tuesday," she said. "Before the fun stuff—any big-deal dilemmas we need to sort?"

"The October issue is going to be too long. Something's going to have to get cut," a guy with dreadlocks and a pink polo shirt said.

I looked around the room at everyone. I saw the nice writer with the shaved head and superhero stickers, and some others who I'd seen at their cubicles. But mostly I saw faces I didn't know.

"Any suggestions?" Akshita asked.

Whitney's and Cailin's eyes followed the voices in the room as the staff threw out ideas. Akshita was at the whiteboard, writing them in black marker.

Harlow raised her hand.

"No need to hand raise, Harlow. Just shout it out," Mindy said from across the table. Her shirt had a picture of a magic lamp.

I liked the idea of a room with no hand raising. A place where you couldn't get caught off guard.

"Sorry." She drew a dot on the notebook page in front

of her, under the words *Staff Meeting*. "Is there a way to tell which sections your readers like the most? Maybe you can cut from their least favorite."

Akshita added Harlow's idea to the list on the board, and Harlow didn't stop smiling through the rest of the meeting, not when the group decided to cut the "What Pizza Topping Are You?" personality quiz, not when Mindy made all ten of her Disney jokes, and not when Akshita said it was time to wrap up. She turned to face us.

"Flyers, our photography, fashion, feature writing, and production departments are open for you to experience today. Pick which one interests you the most, and you'll be matched with a staff member from that department."

"Fashion!" Whitney blurted. The lights above made lines on the shiny material of her shirt.

"Follow Izzy." Akshita pointed across the room to a woman by the door with a white-blond bob, pointy glasses, and a dress with a bunch of silver buttons. One by one the rest of the Flyers left with a staff member, left to do what they'd been chosen to come here to do, until it was just me. The broken piece of this Flyer foursome. The one who didn't fit anywhere.

"What are you thinking, Elena?" Akshita asked. Everyone had filed out of the room except for Mindy, who waited by the door.

Diagnosis: not knowing where you belong.

"I don't know," I answered.

"You must've had some idea what part of the magazine you might be interested in when you applied. What's your favorite aspect?" She took another sip from her mug, and it slurped a little. Seeing someone as glamorous as Akshita slurp their tea cracked my crab shell open a tiny bit.

"I love everything about the magazine." I looked down at the smooth surface of the table. "Honestly, I have no idea why you picked me."

"It was your paper," Mindy said.

"Right. Your writing. It was such a compassionate piece on why you wanted to be a therapist. The *Spread Your Wings* team knew we wanted to meet the person behind it."

My heart fluttered. I felt warm, like the sun had found its way through the crack in my shell. Mindy crossed the room and said something quietly in Akshita's ear. Akshita's palm slapped the table.

"That's perfect." Akshita looked at me. "Elena, we know exactly where we need you."

Treatment: will hopefully be found wherever Akshita is sending me.

Chapter
Nineteen

The Purpose

Mindy led me down the maze of cubicles near the entrance. I saw Harlow in a huddle of writers in rolling desk chairs, her pencil never leaving her notebook. Whitney was in a room full of racks of clothing like the ones from the photo shoot. There was a door farther down labeled PHOTO STUDIO with the door closed, and I imagined Cailin learning about camera angles on the other side.

We stopped at a regular cubicle. I saw a woman not much older than Mindy with bronze skin and flower tattoos up and down her arms. She had a diamond stud in her nose that glinted in the light from her computer. I recognized her from the team meeting. She had sat in the back of the room.

"Hey, Gertrude," Mindy said. Gertrude swiveled in her chair to face us. "This is Elena. She's going to work with you."

Gertrude shook my hand and grinned. There was a tattoo of a violet on her middle finger.

"Super. I'm usually a one-person show back here."

"It's a spectacular show though." Mindy bowed. Gertrude laughed, snorting a little, and took the chair from an empty cubicle for me to sit in. Mindy walked away smiling.

I sat in the chair and looked around. Gertrude had pictures of a gray bulldog tacked to a corkboard and a pale purple cushion on her chair.

"That's Bruno," she said, pointing to the dog pictures. "He's the best boy."

"He's cute." My eyes wandered some more, looking for evidence of what her job at *Spread Your Wings* was.

"Thanks for helping me out," she said.

"What exactly am I helping you with?"

"The Ask Amelia advice column," Gertrude said. She reached under her desk for a yellow shoebox and pulled out a stack of letters, all different sizes and colors. "I'm Amelia."

"Isn't your name Gertrude?"

"Technically. But Ask Gertrude doesn't have quite as much of a ring to it."

It seemed exciting to give yourself a new name, to allow yourself to be a different person, but I wondered if sometimes Gertrude got confused between whether she was supposed to be herself or Amelia. She picked up the first letter from the pile in her lap.

"'Dear Amelia, I just tried out for the basketball team at my school but I didn't make it. I'm really disappointed since I love to play and now have to wait a whole year before I can try out again. Maybe I'm just not good enough. Should I quit? Signed, Bad at Basketball.'" Gertrude looked up. "Any advice?"

I thought about how strange it was that I knew Bad at Basketball's biggest disappointment, but not who they were. My heart clenched as Summer's text flooded into my brain. I knew so many things about Summer. That she had a Truly Happy Dimple, that she watched the sunrise, that running made her feel like she was flying. But I didn't know why our friendship was unraveling like a spool of thread.

"She should keep practicing. She shouldn't quit. Even if she never makes the team, if she loves basketball she should keep playing."

"Agreed," Gertrude said.

I wrote a letter in my head. *Dear Amelia, What do you do when the person you love the most is drifting away?*

Gertrude read letter after letter. I gave advice on failing grades and annoying siblings and fears about starting middle school. I felt myself slip into therapist mode as she typed my ideas as bullet points on her computer. I pictured the writers of the letters on velvet chairs in my future office, not sticky leather couches. I imagined them talking about the tangled parts of themselves, me knowing just the right way to unknot them. Gertrude picked up the next letter.

"'Dear Amelia, I don't know what to do. I've had this best friend for a long time, and I think she might have a secret she's not telling me. We've always been so close. I'm afraid to lose her. Can you help? Signed, Friendless.'"

I stared at a picture of Bruno with a bone in his mouth.

"Elena?" Gertrude probed. "Thoughts?"

The office was full of the sounds of typing, and I was full of the need to help Friendless.

"Just because something has *always* been one way, doesn't mean it always will be. Or that it always should be."

I pulled the advice from a deep part of my heart. The part that wondered if Summer and I would ever be the same again. Gertrude nodded and typed, urged me to keep going.

"They need to talk. Nothing is going to get solved if they don't."

"You're a natural," Gertrude said.

Gertrude added the rest of my advice to Friendless, the advice I wasn't sure I'd be able to take myself. She had a rose on each of her thumbs. The petals nodded in agreement.

Chapter
Twenty

The Check-In

I was still swirling with happiness when we got back to the lobby of the Tappiston after our day at headquarters. We'd eaten lunch in the *Spread Your Wings* cafeteria, which had bright purple bulletin boards with typed-up newsletters and a silver refrigerator stocked with sparkling water. Mindy said all the snacks on the counter were free, so the four of us raided the baskets until we had a mountain of crinkly bags on the table in front of us. Whitney and I shared pretzels on the walk back to the hotel. My hand was in the bag when my phone rang in my pocket. Summer's text flashed through my mind.

"Are you going to get that?" Whitney asked. She licked the salt off a pretzel.

I shook my head and my phone went silent. We were

at the elevator when it started ringing again. The door slid open and the rest of the Flyers got on. I paused outside the door, easing the phone out of my pocket, afraid to look. I breathed a sigh of relief when it was *Mom* on the screen.

"I'll be right up," I said to the Flyers. They disappeared behind the door and I went to sit on the yellow wicker furniture.

"I'm sorry to bug you, Lenny. I know you're busy but I just wanted to hear your voice," Mom said when she answered. The hotel lobby smelled a little like Mom's perfume, but it didn't make me feel homesick. It made me feel like I had a piece of her with me.

"It's okay. Mom, I helped people today. I really helped them. I've always wanted to do that."

Whenever I talk to my mom on the phone, I feel like I can hear her facial expressions through the receiver. She was smiling.

"That's amazing. So you're having a good time?"

I thought of the mound of empty snack bags on the table, the way the sidewalks around the Tappiston Hotel had started to become familiar.

"Yeah, a great time."

Mom cleared her throat. Edgar squealed in the background.

"That must be why Summer says she hasn't heard from you?"

My heart tightened up.

"What do you mean?"

"She came over to babysit Edgar for a few hours today. She seemed down. When I asked what was wrong, she said you were angry with her."

I imagined Summer sitting on our corduroy couch, her legs tucked up under her while she talked to Mom. Mom's hand rubbing comforting circles into Summer's shoulder, even though *I* was the one who deserved the comfort.

"Did she tell you what she said to me?" I asked.

I could hear her squint, lean her head to the side.

"No, but surely it can't be bad enough for you to shut her out entirely. She is your best friend."

"Tell her that."

Eyebrows pulling together.

"What?"

"Tell her that friends don't shut each other out, that they don't treat each other like she's been treating me." My words were coming out as fast as Summer's, an angry stampede of a sentence.

"I'm sure you realize I'm not going to do that, Elena. You need to be the one to talk to her."

Some hotel guests came to gather around the wicker furniture, their conversation so loud I couldn't hear if Mom, or her facial expressions, said anything else.

"Okay. Bye." I hung up and stepped away from all the

chatter. On the ride up to the room the elevator beeped with every passing floor like an accusation. Lyrics popped into my head but I didn't have my Lyric Libro, so I pretended to write them across the air in front of me.

How am I supposed to help,
If I can't even help myself?
How can I save the day,
When I'm a wall in my own way?

Chapter
Twenty-One

The Big Chair

Whitney and I were alone in the room. Cailin and Harlow had gone to the hotel gym. In episode five of *On the Mat* they filmed Cailin's team's workout routine, which involved more push-ups and squats than I'd done in my whole life. Cailin said she did the whole thing once a week. Harlow went with her to observe from the perspective of a sports journalist.

"Dasha Clark had to seriously fight for her sports column in the *Vernon Daily*," Harlow had said before they left.

"Dasha who? The Vernon what?" Whitney asked.

Harlow laughed.

"I forgot to cover the five Ws. Who, what, where, when, why." She shoved her pencil through the dark hair by her ear. "Dasha Clark was a reporter in the fifties at the *Vernon*

Daily, the newspaper in my town. She was the first female reporter in eastern New York, and she was Japanese like me, and therefore she is both my hero and a revolutionary."

"Great word," Cailin said.

I remembered after Summer came in first at the all-county meet, a journalist had interviewed her for the paper, scribbling into a notepad faster than I thought possible. Maybe because Summer was talking so fast. I could picture Harlow as that reporter, her head bent down, taking in every single word.

When Harlow and Cailin were gone, Whitney dragged her duffel bag over to the bed. I was perched on the edge. The TV played a romantic comedy, but I wasn't paying attention to it. Whitney started to pull her clothes out of her bag, piece by piece, and lay them on the comforter. She assembled the outfits like puzzles.

"You're so good at that," I told her.

"At what?" she asked. On a black dress she laid a long gold necklace with a heart-shaped locket.

"Clothes. Putting outfits together. Everything you wear is perfect."

"Oh." Whitney looked down at the outfits with her forehead wrinkled up, like she was noticing them for the first time. "Yeah, it's important to me."

In one ear I heard the movie, the guy character professing their love. In the other I heard Whitney's breathing turn rough like in Grand Central.

"Are you feeling . . . like before?" I asked.

Whitney picked the gold necklace back up.

"No, I'll be fine if I can get this right." She moved the necklace from outfit to outfit, her fist bouncing against the mattress. I watched the charm on the necklace slide across the chain.

"It goes with all of them. I mean it."

She stopped, then placed the necklace back on the black dress where it started.

"I'm just worried about the outfits I helped with earlier for the issue. They're not good enough."

The sensation I'd had at headquarters with Gertrude settled over me. I focused on Whitney's feelings, her sharing the most important thing going on in her world. Like flowers that needed care, and I was the one who could help. I knew Whitney's diagnosis: panic. And now I knew that fashion was her treatment.

"Do you feel like if your outfit lines up, it lets your thoughts line up too?"

Whitney's head lifted. A loose curl hung across her glasses.

"It's like you read my mind or something." She sat on the edge of Cailin and Harlow's bed and observed her work. "Do you want to know what it feels like?"

I nodded and sat across from her on our bed. On the TV the love interest couldn't decide if she was in love or not.

"Near where I live in Philly, there's this giant red chair
down by the water. It looks like a normal wooden lawn chair,
but it's big enough for a bunch of people to sit in. It's supposed to be cute or touristy or whatever. Me and my friends
Paige and Monique went to sit in it, and they were laughing
and stuff. Cause it's a giant chair. But I started having this
explosion inside. My heart and lungs, all of me just got so
scared of being so small compared to something so big."

"I get it," I said.

"Do you? I feel like it makes no sense."

"No one wants to feel small."

Whitney stood and wrapped her arms around me, her
breath even now. She smelled like coconut sunscreen.

The hotel door whirred and Cailin and Harlow came
in. Cailin crouched and did a diving forward roll across the
entryway. She ended up sprawled on her back in the space at
the foot of the beds. Harlow followed behind, writing into
her notebook.

"That's an entrance," she said.

"I always get a little wired after a workout," Cailin
answered. Her eyes spun around as she watched the palm
frond fan blades on the ceiling fan. She'd wiped off her
makeup before the gym, and without it I could see a sprinkle
of freckles on her nose.

"I'm the opposite. I collapse into a heap on the floor,"
Whitney said. She sat next to me on the bed.

"Well, we both end up on the floor, so we're not too different." Cailin laughed. She sat up, facing the desk, and gasped. "How did I not notice these before?"

She picked up a basket of mints on the desk.

"Housekeeping must have left them," Harlow said. "What was that jump you did with your legs straight out called again?"

"A pike. But that's not important right now. Do you know what these are?" Cailin took a mint from the basket and held it out to us, acting like it was a diamond and not a chalky white mint.

"A Wint-O-Green Life Saver?" Whitney answered.

"No, these are magic. Come on." She tossed me the mint and I caught it. The wrapper was warm from Cailin's palm. When she'd given one to Harlow and Whitney, Cailin pushed us all into the bathroom and closed the door.

"Is this some kind of cheerleading initiation? Because I saw what you made new members do in *On the Mat* and I am not getting into an ice bath," Harlow said. She hopped up to sit on the edge of the sink. Whitney took the spot next to her. I stood against the wall by the tub.

"This will be our Flyers initiation. Repeat after me." She popped the mint into her mouth and chewed hard with her mouth open, the mint making cracking sounds. Her face contorted as she crunched and smiled at the same time. It occurred to me that I'd never seen Cailin look less than perfect. On TV and on her profile she was pretty and put together, the spokesperson for Sunny Days Gel Polish, the girl in the Miami sun. Now her features were squished and spit flew out of her mouth.

"I'm so confused," Whitney said.

"Just trust me."

The rest of us put the mints in our mouths and started chomping. Cailin turned the light off. Pitch black fell over the room. I looked around the dark to the spots where I knew the Flyers were sitting. Tiny blue lights ignited where their faces should be.

"What is that?" I asked through the minty crumbs in my teeth.

"Wint-O-Green Life Savers make sparks!" Cailin answered.

"Magic is the only explanation for this," Whitney said.

"It must be something in the flavoring," Harlow responded.

"No. I agree. It's magic," I said.

We laughed and chewed in the dark, the sparks like little stars. I memorized every detail of the moment. The mints cracking. The way it was like our laughter created light.

Chapter
Twenty-Two

The Park

Central Park was like its own little universe. The tall buildings and brick town houses with flower-filled window boxes turned into a sea of grass and sidewalks. Mindy told us the park stretched across nine neighborhoods, and I liked the idea that you could be lost in lots of places and still find your way here.

It had rained overnight, so there were puddles on the sidewalks and the air smelled clean. The itinerary for Wednesday told us we'd spend the morning writing in the park. We walked with our bags full of paper and pens, past a fountain, a playground, and at least fifty dogs. James took a picture of us in front of a fountain with an angel on top. Harlow kept looking at the angel after we were done with the picture. She stuck her finger into the pool of water and swirled it around, the corners of her mouth turned down.

"What's wrong?" Whitney asked her. She wore a thick flowery headband that matched her slip-on sneakers.

Harlow squinted up at the angel, at its creased copper gown.

"The statue reminds me of one that used to be in my town. In front of the *Vernon Daily* building."

"It was an angel?" Cailin added. We started walking again and crossed paths with a group of kids who looked our age. They stared wide-eyed at Cailin and whispered behind their hands. Cailin pushed her sunglasses down off the top of her head.

"It was of Dasha Clark. There were benches all around it that I'd sit on after school and work on my stories for journalism class. I'd try to channel her energy while I wrote."

Harlow wiped her wet hand off on her shorts and it left a rainbow-shaped mark behind.

"There it is," Mindy said, and pointed toward a red checkered blanket set up in the grass. The blanket had plates spread out around a wooden cutting board covered in wedges of yellow and white cheese, round crackers, and condiment cups full of dark pink jelly. If there was ever a picnic that belonged in the pages of a magazine, it was this one. James took a picture of the setup and then flipped his camera around to show Cailin.

"What do you think?"

Cailin looked back and forth between the camera and the park, squinting toward the sky.

"Can you get more sunlight? Like, not enough to wash it all out but just enough to make it . . . glow?" She wiggled her fingers when she said "glow." She'd reapplied her Sunny Days Gel Polish that morning and took a picture of her hand wrapped around her MetroCard. She captioned it *my Sunny Days goes where I go.*

"You got it, girl." James moved to the left side of the checkered blanket and took another shot.

As we sat, Mindy told us to take out our notebooks and sliced a piece of cheese from one of the wedges. The little flag attached to a toothpick stuck into it said *Brie.*

"Itinerary spoiler alert—you'll be finishing your Flyer essays on Friday. But we're not going to have you go into that cold. Today's the day for first drafts, word vomit, drawing pictures of castles, whatever it is you need to do."

Harlow snapped a long, crunchy breadstick in half without looking at it. Her eyes were on the angel statue. We could only see its wings from here. I took a piece from the wedge labeled *Cheddar.* My abuelita uses cheddar for her empanadillas, and the taste was like being with her, rolling out dough in our kitchen.

"We're going to do what's called a sprint. That's five minutes of nonstop work. Whatever spills out, let it spill, just keep your pencil moving." Mindy clicked a button on her watch. "Go."

The rest of the Flyers' pencils jumped to action right away. I pressed the tip to the paper, my mind as blank as the sheet. Pressure climbed up in my chest. I wanted multiple choice questions, an essay prompt, a fill-in-the blank section with a word bank. There were too many things that could spill out onto this empty space. Too many thoughts about Summer and everything that had happened between us.

Summer, I wrote. *I thought we were our own galaxy, the two of us. But it hasn't been like that lately. We're not the friends I thought we were. Not since Joey's party, or the locker room, or the bus ride to the winter field trip to the tree farm.*

We'd gotten our ears pierced together at Farrah's in the mall the week before. It was my first piercing, and your second. The needle hurt more than I thought it would but then it was over, and I inspected the little diamond in the mirror. I liked how it made my whole face look brighter, like a social media filter in real life. You wanted us to wear matching silver hoops to the tree farm. The piercer at Farrah's had said not to swap out the earrings for a few weeks, but I wanted to match you too, so I took the diamonds out and replaced them with the hoops. I pressed the sharp end of the earring into my still-healing earlobe. The pain was enough to make me suck in my breath, and it still hurt when we climbed onto the bus for the field trip. I ignored it. Because our silver hoops were the same, and we were sitting next to each other, and that made things better.

Until Kendra leaned over the seat.

"Elena, I didn't know you were an alien," she said.

A blush shot into my cheeks. My mouth went dry.

"What?" I managed to croak.

"Your ears are green." Her voice was louder now. Loud enough to make you and our other classmates sitting nearby turn their heads. Sara popped up next to Kendra.

"And bleeding. The transformation to alien must be painful."

I put a hand to my ear. When I pulled away, there was a smear of blood on my fingertip.

"It's just the. Um. Metal. A reaction to the metal in the earring," I said. I had read the instructions and cautions on the bottle of cleaning solution. It warned this could happen, it just didn't mention the hazard of it happening on a school bus.

"Nah, I think you're part Martian." Kendra said "Martian" in a pinched voice that made some kids in the other seats laugh.

I waited for you to say something, Summer. Tell everyone that we'd gotten our ears pierced together last week, and squeezed each other's hands when the needle went through, but you didn't. Your nose wrinkled.

"It does look pretty gross," you said.

Kendra and Sara giggled and sunk back into their seat behind us. I undid the clasps on the hoops and pulled them out of my ears, stuck them into a deep pocket of my backpack. Then I made sure my hair was covering the sides of my face so no one would be able

to see my ears anymore. I could barely look at you for the rest of
the bus ride, or while we walked around the tree farm. But you
chattered like nothing had happened. You never said you were
sorry, and your silver hoops sparkled like the drops of frost on the
pine trees.

I guess what I'm trying to say is we're not in the same galaxy
at all. We're in completely different universes.

"Freeze!" Mindy shouted. Her watch beeped to the tune of "Part of Your World" from *The Little Mermaid*.

I looked down at my sheet and didn't recognize the words, like they'd come from a part of myself I didn't know existed. I wanted to throw the whole thing away. Discard it like all the texts I'd drafted to Summer and then deleted.

"That was fun," Whitney said. She flipped her notebook around to show us. She'd sketched out an outfit. A flowy tank top with a knot at the waist, shorts with lacy fringe, a pair of high-top sneakers. "I don't know how this will turn into an essay, but I may have just designed my outfit for the first day of school."

"First day of school outfit. Back-to-school September issue of *Spread Your Wings*. *Spread Your Wings* essay. It all connects," Mindy said. She poked her temple. "That's what sprinting is about. Anyone else want to share?"

In the trees birds sang songs that sounded sort of like *speeeak*. I pressed my notebook into my chest and grabbed another bite of cheddar so my mouth was too full to read what I'd written. The heat in my cheeks was turning me as pink as the raspberry jelly. Cailin took a picture of the corner of the picnic blanket, where it turned from red and white checkers to thick green grass. We sat close enough for me to see her post the picture. It wasn't what she usually posted to her page. I wondered why she'd chosen to do so now.

"I'll go," Harlow said. She cleared her throat. "'There was a crime committed at the *Vernon Daily* newspaper building on the night of June twenty-first. The statue of Dasha Clark, placed in the lawn after her death five years ago, was vandalized. Spray paint was the method of destruction. The crime was committed by four teenagers who legally cannot be identified here. The motive for their destruction is unclear, and as a reporter who used to sit in the shade on the benches surrounding the statue, I am left bewildered by what has been done. It was my place of inspiration. Now it's gone.'"

Everything was quiet when she finished, except for the birds.

"Is that true?" Cailin asked.

"Of course it's true," Harlow answered, her voice thick. "I only report the truth."

Diagnosis: the loss of something you loved. Treatment: write about it. Hope that some of the bad feelings get left on the page.

Harlow reached down for a breadstick, but instead of eating it, she stuck it behind her ear. Whitney burst out laughing and Harlow stared at her.

"What?" she asked.

"You just put the breadstick behind your ear instead of a pencil." She reached toward Harlow, into her wispy dark hair, and pulled the skinny stick out.

Harlow cracked up and the rest of us joined in. James took pictures until we stopped.

Mindy had us do more writing exercises, but we mostly laughed and devoured the cheese board and lay back in the thick grass. The birds kept singing.

On our walk to the hotel I fell behind so I could look at Cailin's page. I wanted to see the picture of the checkered blanket and the grass she'd posted. I wondered what kind of comments her followers would leave about the piece of our picnic. But the picture wasn't there.

Chapter
Twenty-Three

The Fall

Mindy told us we had an hour to get ready for what she called our "Flyer gourmet dinner experience." I wouldn't have minded delivery pizza in our hotel room again, but a fancy dinner out in the city could be fun. I imagined all of us eating on a garden terrace, twinkle lights and woven vines mixed in a leafy green canopy above our heads. The only leafy canopy in our room was the palm frond fan blades on the ceiling, whirling around and around.

I lay on top of our bed and watched it spin. The light coming in from the window was bright gold.

"It looks like a bomb went off in here," Whitney said, walking out of the bathroom. She wore black jeans with an olive-green tank top tucked in. "And we are the bombs."

"The messier you are around someone the more you like

them," Cailin answered, sorting through her makeup bag on the dresser. It was black with a red rhinestone *C*.

"Fact," Harlow said, holding up a finger. She sat cross-legged on the other bed and smiled at the pages of her tiny notebook.

"We must really like each other then," I said without thinking whether it was my turn to talk. It just felt like it was. It felt like in this group of the four of us there were places where I fit.

After we got dressed, we all ended up at the long bathroom counter together.

"Try this," Cailin said to me, and handed over a shiny tube of pink lip gloss. "It'll look good on you."

I took it, pinching the tube between my fingers; it all felt normal. Like we had been friends for years instead of days. Real friends, not just Flyer friends. Friends who shared things. Happiness exploded in my chest like fizzy bubbles.

Whitney inched a tan belt through the loops on her jeans and buckled it. A second later she shook her head and took the belt off, dropping it on the floor.

"What makes you like fashion so much?" Harlow asked. She was dressed in her resporty style, a blue blazer over her Yankees shirt and the same khakis she'd worn to Central Park.

I wondered if Whitney would tell Harlow the truth—about how the perfect outfit made her thoughts settle down.

Whitney pulled a floral scarf out of her bag on the floor and started easing it through the loops. She tilted her head in the mirror.

"The way I see it, I have one small piece of this world. And I want to decorate it the best I can. Make it something beautiful."

"I love that," Cailin said.

"Yeah, thanks . . ." Whitney's voice trailed off. She knotted the scarf at her waist. When she was done, she snapped her head back up. "Getting ready like this reminds me of those shots of you and your teammates before competitions."

Cailin held a mascara wand up to her eyes.

"It's kind of like this. Except your body doesn't know whether to be nervous or excited, and you keep thinking of all the things that could go wrong." She blinked into the wand and coated her lashes in black. "There's also more glitter. *A lot* of glitter. And hairspray."

We laughed. Harlow put her brush down on the counter and gathered her hair to the side.

"What was it like when it did go wrong?" she asked.

"It was . . ." Cailin trailed off.

Summer and I had watched, gripping the edge of the sofa while Lone Star Elite's routine started, perfect at first. Then Cailin's stunt group hoisted her up into the air, and instead of Cailin's legs staying straight and sturdy, they bent. She crumbled, her group catching her in a cradled position, the big smiles falling off their faces. I felt my palms go sweaty now just thinking about it, still holding Cailin's lip gloss tube.

"Freeing."

Whitney's eyes shifted to Cailin in the mirror. I unscrewed the top of the lip gloss and my head filled with the artificial strawberry scent. After that competition, when her team walked away with the fourth-place trophy, the camera followed Cailin but she wouldn't turn around. She kept her red sunglasses on.

"You were happy about it," Harlow stated like it was a fact. She tied her inky black hair to the side and used silver clips to make it stay.

"I wasn't happy." Cailin snapped the mascara shut. She put it back in the makeup bag and pulled out a bottle of perfume. "I'm an athlete. I didn't want to lose. But the pressure was finally gone. I went into every competition knowing I'd never fallen before. Now I had. It took the weight away."

"That makes sense," Whitney said.

Harlow shook her head.

"Not really, though, because at your team meeting you said falling was what you were most afraid of."

"How much sense would it have made to the story if I said it was a relief to fall?" Cailin pressed the nozzle on the perfume and the liquid shot out in a flowery-sweet mist.

Harlow pushed in her last clip.

"It's *your* story. It doesn't have to make sense as long as it's the truth."

I swiped the lip gloss across my mouth and put it back in Cailin's bag. The motion made it tip, and a bottle of lavender Sunny Days Gel Polish rolled out. Harlow had been so upset when Cailin revealed that the polish didn't really last.

"It's not always that simple, Harlow," Whitney said.

I thought about Whitney's secret panic attacks, and a pit formed in my stomach.

"Sometimes it is." Harlow's eyes were full of hurt when she walked out of the bathroom, and the pit in my stomach turned to suspicion; I had an inkling that Harlow wasn't talking about Cailin anymore.

Chapter Twenty-Four

The Gourmet Experience

Harlow seemed less angry on the way to dinner. She told us a story about Francine Mayfield, a woman who lived in Vernon, New York, for all ninety-six years of her life. The *Vernon Daily* had run an article about her. She made funny needlepoints and sold them online. She stitched words like *TGIF, Not Listening,* and *Every Day Is Taco Tuesday If You Believe.* According to Francine the general public deserved more from needlepoint than flowers. Harlow saved up her money to buy one that said *Don't Waste My Time,* and when she went to hang it on the wall, she noticed the underside. The thread was messy and knotted. The words were fuzzy, backward, and unrecognizable. I walked behind her, next to Whitney, and thought about how things usually look different from the other side.

La Rosa Fine Italian was a few blocks from the hotel. When we got inside, the host waited behind a stand that looked like a marble column. He wore a vest and had shoulder-length brown hair. He led us to a table in the center of the restaurant with a little *Reserved* card on it. Akshita was there, and a long-stemmed rose stretched across each of our red placemats. The thorns had been picked off.

"What about menus?" Harlow asked while the host filled our glasses with water. The ice cubes clinked together.

"La Rosa put together a fixed menu for us," Akshita said from the end of the table. She wore an almond brown dress. "Three courses."

Cailin picked up her rose and twirled it between her fingers. She captured the movement with a video on her phone. The stem spun, the petals splaying out each time. The host and another server, a girl with a tight ponytail, came back and dropped a basket of bread on each end of the table. Mindy clapped her hands from the spot next to Akshita. I wondered if she felt like she was in *Beauty in the Beast*, and the candle in the center of the table was going to come to life and sing "Be Our Guest."

Whitney handed me a roll before lowering her head to say grace. I tore it open, expecting steam and the floury smell of a bakery. Instead the roll stretched open like chewed gum. The inside looked like it had never seen an oven.

"Does it seem a little doughy to you?" Harlow leaned in

to whisper in my ear. She sliced a slab of butter off with her knife and spread it inside the bread.

"It's made of dough," I answered.

"I mean uncooked."

"My abuelita lets me eat the raw dough when she makes empanadillas. It's like eating goo," I said, and took a bite. It was tough and sticky in my mouth.

"What about foodborne illness?" Harlow asked, louder this time. Cailin and Whitney stopped mid-bite.

"Foodborne what?" Cailin asks.

"Food poisoning."

"I never got food poisoning from it," I said.

"Hey, Flyers," Mindy said. "Let's stop talking about food poisoning at the four-star restaurant."

I put my uneaten roll down on the small plate at my setting. I noticed Cailin take a picture of her line of utensils, the phone held close to the polished knife.

Akshita cleared her throat.

"I like to use the Flyers dinner as a check-in point," she said. "How is everyone so far?"

"Amazing," Whitney answered. She laid her cloth napkin on her lap.

"I'm glad. Any highlights? Anyone?"

"James let me use his camera at the donut shop," Cailin said. She took another picture, this time of the salad fork.

"Making sparks with the Life Savers," I added.

The other Flyers nodded like they agreed. I felt bright and shiny, lit like the tall white candle in the middle of the table.

Akshita smiled.

"It's often the moments the magazine doesn't get to see that become favorites," she said.

We added a few more highlights to the list, like eating the cheese board while sprawled out in the grass in Central Park, and the day of the staff meeting, before garden salads were delivered to the table.

Grape tomato halves and chunks of cucumbers were spread on a bed of romaine with thick slices of mozzarella. The whole affair dripped with balsamic vinaigrette dressing. I scrunched my nose. Balsamic reminded me of muddy footsteps on a floor. Everyone dug into the soggy salad. I picked up my fork and took a delicate bite, because I didn't want to complain. The sour taste of balsamic tortured my tongue. Harlow picked wrinkled tomatoes out of hers and left them in a semicircle around her plate.

"Do you like it?" I whispered to Whitney.

"It has walnuts in it," she said, moving the salad around with her fork.

"Does that mean yes?"

"It means it's classy. My parents take me to this fully vegetarian salad restaurant every year for my birthday, and the one with the walnuts and grapes in it is called the Class Act."

"When's your birthday?" I asked.

"March sixteenth."

"You're a Pisces," I said, and smiled at the slimy salad. Pisces had a fish as their symbol. I imagined Whitney's Pisces fish swimming alongside my Cancer crab.

"Is that a good one?" Whitney asked. I nodded, and she picked one of the walnuts out of the salad and ate it.

The spaghetti came out next, picture perfect and flecked with oregano. My stomach groaned like it was saying *thank you, finally*. Akshita picked up her water glass and held it toward us.

"Every Flyer experience is different," she said. "But we hope you are loving yours. Cheers." We all said "cheers" too and took a sip from our fancy drinks. I'd ordered the apple cider, and it came with a cinnamon stick straw that reminded me of autumn. It was spicy and sweet. Whitney's lemonade had a pineapple slice on the rim, and Harlow and Cailin both had Shirley Temples full of maraschino cherries.

I put my chilled glass down and took a bite of the pasta. It clumped in my mouth, somehow slimy and dusty at the same time. The sauce had a sharp, salty bite that lingered even after I chugged half my cider.

I looked at everyone else eating. Cailin held up her fork with spaghetti twirled around it. The pasta looked like something on the cover of a food magazine. She took a picture.

"Are you for real?" Harlow asked. She glared at Cailin.

Cailin put the tightly swirled bite back down.

"I have no idea what you're talking about."

"You must have some deal with this restaurant because the food is disgusting and you're still going to post a picture like it's not."

"Whoa, Harlow," Whitney mumbled under her breath.

"You don't know what I was doing," Cailin snapped.

"I do actually. You're lying to your followers."

Akshita cleared her throat and held up her hand.

"Take a breath, guys," Whitney said.

Harlow turned to Whitney.

"You're not much better. You have a secret too. And you." Harlow pointed at me with her fork, eyes like wildfire, out of control. "You barely say anything."

I stared out toward the rest of the dining room, so I wouldn't have to watch Harlow accuse me of things I already knew. It didn't look like a fancy restaurant anymore. The paintings and sconces on the walls were like the tacky decorations in the haunted house Franklin City sets up in the fall. I imagined cobwebs hanging off the fireplace, the host jumping out from behind the marble pillar and yelling "boo" in a monster mask.

Summer and I always do the haunted house together. We link our arms while scarecrows and zombies come to life. We had a million memories like that but they were murky now, like looking through seaweed in the water.

"But you're the worst one, Cailin. You post pictures about how you love all this stuff but it's not true, you're just selling it. And you made everyone think you were torn up about falling on TV when you were glad you did." Her voice broke on the word *glad*.

Cailin's hand wrapped around her fork and her mouth opened like she was going to respond.

"Enough," Akshita said, loudly enough to catch our attention but quiet enough to not draw the notice of the entire restaurant. "Do you think we choose Flyers who are all the same? No. We want our Flyers to be different. To have different points of view. Different experiences. Not everyone may feel the same way you do. And judging and criticizing them is not constructive."

Harlow stared at the candle while her face turned burnt red. Her eyes pooled with tears and the sharp lines of her cheeks wobbled.

"Sorry," she said, her voice thick.

The waiter came over again and stopped short when he took in the scene. Plates of uneaten spaghetti, the last few days shattered like pieces of glass all over the table.

"We'll take dessert to go," Akshita said.

I thought about Harlow's story of the underside of a needlepoint. Maybe magazine internships are like that. Pretty and polished from the outside while covering up the ugly truth. Maybe this was the case for friendships, too.

Chapter Twenty-Five

The Aftermath

The hotel room was cold from the air-conditioning, and the TV was on from before we left for dinner. Cailin's makeup bag sat on the dresser, its colorful tubes spilling onto the wood. It was the worst kind of before and after. Before, we laughed and shared lip gloss. After, we sat in bed, quiet.

The Devil Wears Prada played on the TV.

"Imagine if Akshita went full Miranda Priestly on us," Whitney said, and looked back and forth between the beds.

"Miranda is cutthroat but she really just has high standards," Cailin said. She had the spare blanket from the closet wrapped around her shoulders. "My coach can be like that. It stings in the moment but makes you stronger in the end."

On the screen Miranda's assistant, Emily, got hit by a car. I flinched.

"Can we just go to bed?" Harlow threw the covers over her head and faced the wall.

Whitney sighed and pressed the power button on the remote. The TV screen went black before Andy could tell Emily she was taking her spot in Paris. Cailin shifted around in the other bed and mumbled "good night" into her pillow. I slowly lay down, toward the window, facing the lights outside. I tried not to smell the berry lip gloss or the slight scent of pizza from a night that wasn't like this one. I didn't turn back around to see all of us curled up like tiny, lonely islands.

My phone vibrated on the nightstand. I grabbed it before the sound could disturb anyone and held it close to my face. A message from Summer floated on the home screen.

I'm sorry, Elena.

I clicked the button to turn the screen black again, then put the phone facedown on the nightstand. I squeezed my eyes shut against hot tears. Before this week I would've told Summer that all was forgiven. But I could feel it, the way we'd changed this year, and it wouldn't be fixed with one text. I had to talk to her about it. But how?

Chapter
Twenty-Six

The Cave

James met us in front of the Tappiston the next morning. Mindy had filled up the quiet spaces during breakfast talking about our trip to the aquarium, the first item on that morning's itinerary. We had to take the subway, and it was crowded and warm in the terminal. The halls opened up into the area for swiping MetroCards. Off to the side a woman in a long green dress and knit cap stood with a guitar. Her black hair almost touched the strings while she strummed and sang, her voice filling up the terminal. I didn't recognize the song and I wondered if she'd written it herself.

"She's good," Cailin said. She was in front of me in the line to get through the turnstiles. The woman had her guitar case open in front of her, and some people put dollar bills inside.

"Yeah," I said. My voice was almost a whisper. I wanted to stay and listen. I wanted to ask her how she was brave enough to sing when people were looking.

"Elena." Harlow was behind me. She pointed ahead. I was holding up the line. I slid my card through the sensor and pushed through the metal bar. We walked down the platform until I couldn't hear the singing anymore.

There were too many people on the subway for us to sit together, so we found seats spaced out from one another. I saw James move his camera around like he was trying to find an angle that would capture all of us, but he lowered it eventually, frowning at the display.

There was a section of the aquarium kept dark, and the fish tanks glowed with white-blue light. In the center was a tank made to look like a coral reef. Bright yellow flounders darted through rocks and angelfish swam, their fins like long white hair. Mindy was friends with the employee watching the touch tank and stayed to talk to him. Every few minutes he'd stop their conversation to deliver a fact about one of the animals.

"Can anyone tell me what sea cucumbers eat?" he asked. He adjusted the collar on his mustard-colored polo. *Pedro* was stitched into the fabric under the aquarium logo.

"Algae," I whispered to myself. I'd learned the fact in earth science.

"What was that?" Pedro asked. I glanced around the

touch tanks to find who he was talking to, but everyone else's eyes were on me. I waited for my skin to burst into flames, my throat to squeeze so tight no words could come out. But it didn't happen. The water in the touch tanks rippled and the lights were dark, and in my head was the yellow poster board Summer and I had put together in earth science, with facts about the sea cucumber's diet glued onto the right side.

"Algae," I repeated, loud enough this time for everyone to hear.

"Right."

Pedro went back to talking to Mindy and everyone else went back to dipping their hands into the water, and nothing bad had happened because I'd spoken up. Maybe someone even knew something they hadn't known before because of what I'd said. I wandered over to a tank of clownfish. It reminded me that soon I would be back home, and Edgar's fish movie would be on. Things had gotten so messy here, but I wasn't ready to leave. I heard a click and saw James nearby. He checked his camera and gave me a thumbs-up. I looked back to the fish and thought that this week away from home was a little like being in a tank. The world was starting to distort. But not in a bad way.

I walked toward the sound of Cailin's voice. She was with Harlow in front of a tank with murky water. When I got closer, I saw a starfish pressed to a flat rock inside.

"Are you ready to stop hating me?" Cailin asked. She

stared at Harlow while Harlow stared at the starfish. Neither of them seemed to notice me.

"I don't hate you," she answered, her voice even.

"You fully flipped out on me. I wasn't even taking a picture of the food or the restaurant or whatever. I liked how the light looked from the candle. And now you won't even let me explain."

Harlow finally turned away from the tank.

"I don't want to talk about it. I just want everyone to stop acting like things are so great when they're not. I want everyone to be honest."

"I told you all about me falling because I wanted to be *honest*," Cailin said. "No one sees me as a real person anymore. I wanted you all to, at least."

I thought about Summer. The boat launch. Antarctica.

"When you're somewhere no one knows you, you can be anyone you want," I said.

Cailin and Harlow turned their heads like they were just realizing I was there. The starfish slid from the rock to the black floor of the tank.

"What did you say?" Cailin asked.

I repeated it, the words Summer had said to me on the dock.

"That's exactly how I felt. I didn't want to come here and be Magnet. I wanted to be Cailin."

In my head, I thought, *I wish Whitney were here,* so she

could see the ice melt away between Cailin and Harlow. And then I realized I hadn't seen her in a while.

"Has anyone seen Whitney?"

Cailin and Harlow shook their heads. I looked around the dark room, past the coral reef tank and the kids on summer camp field trips in matching shirts. Whitney wasn't anywhere.

"We should find her," I said, and the three of us split up. Cailin went to tell Mindy. I walked around the edges of the room, my eyes searching the dim lighting for Whitney's high side ponytail, the glare from her glasses, her smile.

There was a hole cut into the wall, painted around the edge to look like a cave. A sign said kids could pass through and experience the ocean floor. The light inside was dim yellow and the carpeted floor was green. I got down on my hands and knees and crawled in.

"Whitney?" I called out softly, then listened. There were posters on the wall about different species of fish, what they ate and their methods of self-defense. I called out her name again.

I heard the sharp wheezing, her crackled voice whispering "over here." I crawled faster, the carpet burning my knees until I found her at the curve of the tunnel in front of a poster about cuttlefish, blocky bubble letters saying they defend themselves through camouflage.

"Are you having a panic attack?"

She nodded. She had her head pressed against the wall and her eyes wide open. Her hair was in a pile on top of her head, her knees tucked into her chest.

"Everything's okay. You're here, at the aquarium, and everything's fine."

She nodded again, more frantically this time. I wondered if I should go get Mindy or James to help, but I couldn't leave her alone.

I heard the shuffling sounds of other people crawling into the tunnel and braced myself for a flock of younger kids to race through. Whitney squeezed herself into a smaller ball, her breaths coming too quick for her to get enough air. I reached out and grabbed her hand.

"There you are," Cailin said, a grin breaking out on her face and then disappearing. She stopped short, which made Harlow crawl into Cailin's butt and the two of them tip into the wall.

A small, shrill laugh mixed in with Whitney's breathing.

"What's going on?" Harlow asked, righting herself back into a sitting position.

"I'm a tiny little fish in a giant ocean," Whitney heaved out. Her head fell and her arms dropped to her sides. I let go of her hand. "How do I not let it swallow me up?"

I thought about the big red chair that made Whitney panic.

"You aren't small, Whitney," I said. "You decorate your

space in the world, just like you said. And it's as big and beautiful as the ocean."

Harlow and Cailin nodded in agreement in the shadows.

Diagnosis: things aren't always pretty. Or as perfect as they seem. Life has storms sometimes.

I reached out and took Whitney's hand again. I held it tight like I had in Grand Central. Cailin and Harlow took the other, all of us connected.

Treatment: sit with the people who care about you, until it passes.

The Profile

Mindy took us back to Lot 88 after the aquarium to take our picture for the cover of the magazine. I kept my eyes on Whitney while we rode the subway. After we'd all crawled out of the tunnel, Mindy was there waiting, and Whitney explained what had happened. Mindy pulled her into a hug and said what she went through was so normal, and asked if she wanted to call her parents. Whitney said no at first but changed her mind when we got outside in the sun. She called her parents by the sea lion exhibit. The rest of us stood close by. When she came back over to us, her face was calm, and she still had that peaceful look now as we took the yellow line to the studio.

We walked through the doors of Lot 88, and I noticed the construction out front was gone. Inside, the same white tarp was hung by the cameras, and the long table was set up but there were no props. Mindy brought us over to the table, and I saw it was covered in printed pictures instead. The pictures we'd taken on our first day to represent us. I wanted to close my eyes. Usually pictures showed me all the things I didn't want to see, like the jeans I'd ripped with Summer. But these were different. My eyes didn't go straight to my curves. They fell on my smile, on the microphone cord coiled up on the ground, on the pink skirt of the dress billowing like I was in front of a fan.

"We look happy," Cailin said.

She sounded surprised.

"I have been happy," I said. I looked at a picture where my eyes were sort of closed and the microphone was close to my mouth, like I'd reached the biggest part of the song.

"The whole time?" Cailin asked.

There'd been not so great parts of the week. But I'd still been excited to read the itinerary in the café every morning. I'd still felt myself crawl further out of my crab shell, inch by inch.

"The whole time," I said.

Everyone squint-smiled down at the pictures like they were trying to see things from a new angle. At our feet a crack ran like a lightning bolt down the concrete floor. I watched Cailin take a picture of it.

"Where do you post those pictures?" I asked.

Her eyes widened and her fingers stopped moving over the screen.

"On my page," she answered.

My chest tightened a little. The pictures I'd watched Cailin take, the ones that weren't of her or Sunny Days Nail Polish, weren't on her page. Not the lifeguard ring, or the forks from the restaurant, or the spot where the checkered picnic blanket turned to grass. I'd looked.

"My photography page," she continued. She pressed the screen a few times, her mouth in a straight line and eyes focused, then turned the phone to the rest of us. "It's called 'The Everyday.' No one knows about it. No one knows it's me."

Harlow took the phone, and Whitney and I leaned in to look over her shoulder while she scrolled. The feed had pictures of all kinds of flowers, daisies and lilies and puffy white dandelions. There were pictures of wooden fences washed in gold from sunsets. The number of followers was on top of the page—twenty-five. So much lower than the one the world knew about. Harlow clicked on the picture of the lifeguard ring, and the caption said *July 12, #TheEveryday*.

"They're so good," Whitney said.

Cailin thanked her and talked about some of her favorites, pointing to a picture of a teapot. I couldn't take my eyes away from the screen. This was like Cailin's own Lyric Libro. It was the way she saw the world. But in secret, so that the world couldn't see who she really was and judge her for it. Like they did when she was on TV. Like I did.

Chapter
Twenty-Eight

The Unidentified Teen

We ate our signature half-pepperoni, half–green pepper pizza off paper towels in the hotel room that night, all four of us cross-legged on Cailin and Harlow's bed. Harlow had brought her favorite issue of *Spread Your Wings* with her, the September one from two years ago, and we flipped through. The Flyers that year had gone to Rockefeller Center and a planetarium. They peered into the sky through long white telescopes. Harlow had drawn a heart next to a picture of the Flyers at the Donut Hole, and it reminded me so much of Summer and me scribbling on pictures and Post-its that my breath caught in my throat. Her apology text was still unanswered in my phone.

"I can't believe we're leaving soon," Cailin said. She was wearing her Lone Star Elite tank top with the bow on it.

Her hair was down, the red streaks glowing from the lamp next to the bed. She turned the page of the magazine. The essay section was next. It looked like the pages of a notebook, words like real handwriting between the lines. The title on top said, WHAT IT FEELS LIKE.

"I can't believe we still have to write our essays," Whitney replied. Her eyes scanned the words while she chewed on her bottom lip.

"Don't remind me," Harlow said.

We all looked at her with identical expressions. Raised eyebrows, worry lines in our foreheads.

"I thought that's what you were most excited about. You're going to do a piece on that vandalism in your town." Cailin closed the magazine.

"I can't do it." Harlow's voice was low. "It's too complicated."

I waited for the words she wasn't saying. Words like the ones in the Ask Amelia letters.

"What's complicated about it?" I asked. If I'd learned anything from Harlow, it was that the best way to gather information is to ask questions.

Harlow squeezed her eyes shut and dropped her head.

"He knew how much the statue meant to me," she said to her knees.

In Central Park, Harlow said four unidentified teenagers had committed the crime. I pieced the truth together.

Maybe she couldn't name the perpetrators in her story, but that didn't mean she didn't know who they were.

"Your brother," I said.

A sound like a whimper rose from Harlow's throat.

"I heard him sneak in through his window on the night it happened, and I found the paint-stained clothes in his closet the next day."

My heart squeezed, thinking of Harlow finding those clothes, the feeling of betrayal shooting straight through her. I hated that the feeling reminded me of Summer.

"You really are a good investigative journalist," Cailin said.

"I didn't want to be this time. But I needed to know why he did it. So I asked him. And he *lied*." She gritted her teeth hard, like if she didn't she would cry. "The next day the police were at our door. They'd caught him on camera."

Harlow's hair hung down, covering her face. Whitney wrapped an arm around her shoulders.

"He really is a stupid dumb stupidface," Whitney said.

It made Harlow laugh and lift her head a little.

"The whole drive I just kept thinking about it. It filled me up and filled me up and by the time we got here, I was ready to explode." She looked up at Cailin. "Which I did."

Cailin shook her head.

"Don't worry about it. Really."

I thought about how everyone had shared their secrets.

Cailin with her photography page, Whitney's anxiety, Harlow and her brother. I was the only one still locked tight.

"I want to show you something," I said, and before I could talk myself out of it I was at my duffel bag, unraveling the purple notebook from inside my hoodie, opening to the page I'd written on last night, after Summer sent her text, the blue city light coming in through the window. "I like to write songs."

I put my Lyric Libro next to the pizza box and let them read.

I wanted to sail away with you
Because you said you felt like sailing too.
But I don't want to run away anymore.
I want to stay here upon the shore,
Both of us sinking into the sand,
No longer afraid to stand.

I watched everyone's eyes run down the lyrics, once and then again. I wondered what kind of melody the lyrics made in their heads, what it made them feel.

Cailin was the first to look up.

"Can I take a picture of this for 'The Everyday'?" she asked.

I fought the urge to pull the notebook away, hug it safe into my chest.

"I don't think it would fit there," I answered.

"It's about beautiful things in everyday life." She pointed

to the notebook. "Your song definitely qualifies."

Whitney ran her finger over the last line.

"Plus your handwriting is unreal," she said.

I thought about my words on Cailin's photography page, mixed in with the flowers and landscapes. If I was going to be brave like the song said, brave enough to not sail away from hard things, this could be where I started.

"Okay," I said.

Harlow flipped the notebook around so it faced Cailin. I watched her maneuver her phone so it looked at the song from the side, like the words were spilling out onto the page, like my handwritten letters were soldiers marching off into the distance. I looked away when she pressed post. My heart pounded and something rose in my chest, like I might scream or cry or laugh. It wasn't a bad feeling.

A singing competition played on the TV, and the two singers with the lowest scores stood holding hands, awaiting their fate. One was a guy with a banjo and pink hair. The other was tall and tan in a red ballgown.

We went back to eating pizza, and I saw Cailin's phone light up on the bed. It stayed lit, little notifications piling up on the screen. Cailin watched them pop up, one after another, chewing on her bottom lip.

"That's weird," she said.

"What is?" My skin turned to goose bumps, the air-conditioning suddenly too cold, my fingertips numb.

"I don't usually get any notifications on that page." She picked up the phone. I waited for her to tell me everything was fine. Instead her eyes went wide. "Oh no. I'm so sorry, Elena."

The host of the show announced that the banjo player's journey had come to an end.

A buzzing came from the other bed, from my phone on top of the pillow. I picked it up and saw Summer's name flash across the screen.

Chapter
Twenty-Nine

The New Language

Cailin scrambled to the door after me. The phone kept buzzing in my hand.

"I'm seriously so sorry, it was a complete accident," she pleaded. I couldn't see her phone on the bed anymore, but I pictured the screen filling up with more notifications, imagined what the comments would say.

"It's okay." A few more buzzes and the call would go to voicemail. Maybe that would be easier. "I'll be back."

I stepped into the hall and answered the phone.

"Hi," I said.

"Hey." Summer's voice made me want to cry. She sounded like my best friend and a stranger at the same time.

"Hi," I said again. I walked down the hall, past the closed doors. I felt the cold floor through my thin striped socks.

Summer scoffed. "I saw the picture of your poem. I'd recognize your handwriting anywhere."

"It's a song."

"You write songs?"

"Yeah."

I got to the end of the hall, turned around, and started back again.

"And these songs are about me."

"Sometimes."

"You never responded to my text," Summer said.

"I didn't know what to say."

I felt every single mile between us. The distance that had been forming even if we never talked about it.

"You just said it to the whole world on Cailin's page instead." Her words were fast, like always, but every one of them sounded hurt.

"That was an accident."

She sniffed and the moment felt like a breakup scene in a movie. The static in the phone, Summer's sniffles, the feeling of the walls closing in.

"Well, I heard you loud and clear. You don't want to be friends anymore. And I know I was harsh, but that sucks Elena, it really does. I apologized."

The hallway spun. That wasn't what the song was about at all. I just wanted to stop being afraid all the time. Afraid of losing her. Afraid of my own voice.

"Things have been different this year, Summer. It's like I'm not good enough to be your friend anymore. It's like I'm someone you pretend to be friends with but make fun of."

"How could you think that? You're like my whole life, Elena."

There were too many things to say, all of them piling up like the notifications on Cailin's phone.

"But you shut me out when you had your first kiss. You made fun of my piercings on the bus to the tree farm. You've been hanging out with Riah instead of me, and—" I felt my voice ready to break. "I heard you in the locker room with Kendra and Sara. You told them you wanted me to back off."

The line was silent, the space between her and me stretching even further.

"I have to go," Summer said, and the line went dead. I kept the phone to my ear when I dropped down in the middle of the hallway, a few doors away from our room, hoping Summer might come back but knowing she wouldn't.

The door on the left side of me opened and Mindy peeked her head out.

"Everything okay?"

"I don't know," I mumbled.

Mindy came to sit with me on the floor. She wore pajamas with glass slippers on them.

"I heard a little bit. Thin walls," she said.

"I think I just lost my best friend."

Down the hall Whitney's head peeked out from our door, then disappeared back inside.

"Do you want to find her?"

I stared at one of the glass slippers on her pajama pants. A diamond sparkled on the toe.

"What?"

"You say you lost her. Well, maybe she's in the elevator." Mindy pointed behind us, toward the elevator in the middle of the hall. "Or at the pool. Or in an enchanted forest. I bet you can find her."

I snort-laughed.

"I think she's hidden a little better than that."

"How else can I put this?" Mindy clicked her heels together. "I took a Portuguese class last semester. Hardest class I've ever taken. But of course it was, you know? It's a new language. And sometimes, when you get older and you and everyone around you starts learning new things about themselves, people start speaking different languages. And we have to learn to translate."

If the things Summer said about me made up a new language, I wasn't sure it was one I wanted to study.

"What if you can't?" I asked.

Mindy stuck her legs straight out in front of her, matching the way I was sitting.

"It happens. Sometimes people can't speak your new language with you." She tapped her knee against my leg.

"I think you're one of the ones who can."

I stared down at my legs until the plaid fabric blurred.

"What if she doesn't want me to?" The words were small and scared.

"She does." Mindy stood and held out her hand. When I took it, she hoisted me up. "I promise," she added.

I held that with me when we said good night, when I walked back down the hall to the room. I realized I'd walked out without a key, but when I got there, the door was propped open with Cailin's suitcase. Whitney, Harlow, and Cailin were leaned into the headboard together when I walked in, Cailin in the middle with her phone out, the others watching her scroll. She tossed it to the side when I walked in, and scrambled across the bed.

"I'm sorry, Elena. How you showed us your song and I totally ruined it," she said. Everyone's face was serious when I sat at the edge of the bed.

I looked around the room at all the mess and clutter we'd created over the past couple days. At the four of us sitting close together.

"It's okay. I think it needed to happen."

"Cailin's photography page gained a thousand followers in five minutes. We've been watching the numbers go up," Whitney said.

"How?" I asked.

"I put the tag on the song picture, since I thought it was

on the Everyday page. Now everyone can find it," Cailin said.

"Sorry, Cailin."

"Don't be! Everyone loves it," she said, a big smile across her face.

I stopped myself from thinking that Cailin was lucky, lucky that she had followers who loved everything she did, lucky her secrets could come out without everything falling apart. I knew her better now. And not everything was perfect in her world either.

"They're great pictures."

Cailin shook her head.

"Not the pictures, your song! See for yourself."

She grabbed the phone from where she'd thrown it and pulled up the picture, then handed it to me.

The song had over two thousand likes. Comment after comment popped up underneath.

This is so meaningful.

Wow, I can really relate to this.

You should post more of these.

"You're a star, Elena," Whitney said.

I read and read and thought about how if I'd sailed away with Summer, I never would have had this moment.

Chapter Thirty

The Idea

When we got to the *Spread Your Wings* **office the** next morning, Akshita was at the table in a black pantsuit. Her hair was swept into a high ponytail. She smiled when we walked in, but her eyes didn't.

"Good to see you, Flyers," she said. "We have to finish your essays today so please take a seat."

We took the same seats that we had the last time we were here, even though there weren't name tags anymore. Instead there was a tablet at each spot. When I sat down, I saw that it was opened to a blank document, the words *My Flyer Essay* already typed into the header.

"Akshita, I'm sorry about the other night," Harlow said.

"We promise to turn it around for the last day," Cailin added.

Akshita smiled.

"Like I said in my toast. Every Flyer experience is different. That doesn't make one better than the other."

I looked around to my fellow Flyers. We all nodded at each other.

"We also had an idea for the essays," I said.

"What's that?" Akshita asked.

"We want to write it together. One essay from all of us," Whitney added.

Akshita's eyes narrowed like she might say no, and then she stood.

"Brilliant." She got up and grabbed a marker, facing the whiteboard. She wrote *collaboration* in big letters. "Let's brainstorm."

That night we ate dinner with Mindy and James at a Mediterranean restaurant near the Tappiston. The food had all the right flavors, no clumpy pasta or metallic tomato sauce. There was even a garden terrace, and we sat near a bush with purple flowers. When we got back to the hotel, Cailin pulled a jar of clay face mask from her suitcase, and the four of us sat on the floor and caked the pink goo on our faces, the mask cracking on my cheeks every time I laughed. We read the early copy of the August issue we'd been given at headquarters. I was responsible for flipping the pages.

Around midnight we were on the last page of the issue where the horoscopes were.

"Oh hey, I can expect great fortune," Harlow said, pointing to the Libra write-up.

"Do you really believe in those things?" Cailin asked. It made sense she would be skeptical about astrology—she was a Taurus.

I glanced at the Cancer horoscope. *This month will bring great change. Do not try to resist it.*

"I believe in it," I said.

"You know what I believe in?" Whitney asked, standing up from the bed and stomping her foot. We all looked up at her.

"What?" Harlow asked.

"Fashion." Whitney tossed her head back and lifted her arms. She still had little flecks of the pink mask around her temples. She wore a flannel set of pajamas with sheep on them.

"Whitney, you have farm animals on your clothes." Cailin laughed. She sat up cross-legged. I watched her take a picture of our setup on the ground, the sheets spread out like a picnic blanket.

"Not for long." She straightened out her glasses. "Let's have a fashion show."

We all smiled over Whitney's idea and stood up from the sea of sheets. Once our clothes were dumped out onto the bed, we scoured the selection. Harlow ended up in a jersey and jeans. Cailin borrowed Whitney's flowery headband. Whitney saw me studying my pile and reached in, extracting the black dress I'd worn on the first day. On the train ride to New York, and down to the pool, where I'd wondered how I would ever fit in to this group.

When we were dressed, we went out to the hall and turned it into a catwalk, laughing when Cailin did cartwheels down the carpet, and when Whitney strutted like a real runway model. We couldn't contain ourselves when Harlow took her turn, taking the pencil out from behind her ear and pointing at all of us like a scolding teacher.

A door opened down the hall and Mindy stepped out. Her hair was like an orange cyclone.

"You Flyers want to get us kicked out of the hotel on the last night?" She rubbed her eyes.

"Sorry, Mindy," Cailin said.

"We'll go to bed," Harlow said, and we scrambled into the room.

"Ha. Kidding," Whitney whispered just to us.

When I woke up, the alarm clock next to the bed said 5:15 in red block numbers. I looked toward the window. It was dark, with just the smallest bit of purple light coming through. I almost closed my eyes to claim another two hours of sleep before we had to get up, pack, and leave, but instead I got up

and went to the window. The buildings were all black shadows, but the sky was swirled-up blue and pink.

"What are you doing?" Whitney mumbled.

I turned around. She was watching me, her glasses on the
pillow next to her.

"Watching the sunrise. Come see."

"It's so early."

"It's worth it."

She groaned and dropped her head back down, but a second later she was pushing off her blanket. She stood next to
me at the window, adjusting her glasses. The sky was even
brighter, the sun crawling higher, when Cailin came to the
window. Orange had crept in when Harlow joined.

I wondered if what I was doing was wrong. Watching the
sunrise had been something I did with Summer, like going
to the boat launch. But there was lots of room on that dock.
There was room at this window for all of us to stand and
stare straight up at the sky.

Chapter
Thirty-One

The Departure

We said goodbye in the Tappiston lobby. Taxis were coming to take Cailin back to the airport, and Whitney and me to Grand Central. A gray SUV pulled up in front of the hotel.

"My mom is here," Harlow said.

I remembered thinking the lobby was like a castle. If it were a castle, then Harlow would be a knight, leaving to go battle whatever was out there for her. I guess we all were.

The four of us huddled.

"We have to stay in touch," Whitney said. "Through a group chat."

We had to give each other our numbers on the first day in case of emergency, in case of separation, and now we'd use them because we were separating. I wondered when we'd ever be all together again. *If* we ever would be.

"What should we call it?" I asked.

"Akshita's Angels?" Harlow suggested.

"How about the Flyers?" Cailin added.

Harlow's mom rolled down her window outside. She waved at us, her face made of the same features as Harlow's. We were running out of time.

"C-H-E-W," I spelled.

Everyone stared at me.

"Chew?" Whitney asked.

"Cailin, Harlow, Elena, Whitney."

We laughed one last time, and the moment was full of pizza and palm frond fan blades, the trees in Central Park. It was full of face masks and bad spaghetti and Wint-O-Green mints. Secrets.

Whitney's train was departing from tunnel fifteen. Mine was at twenty-seven. We stood in the center of Grand Central where the information booth was, the constellations above our heads again. It felt like so much had changed since the last time we were here, but the stars were still there, the Cancer crab scurrying across the blue. I wondered what my horoscope said today. *You will have to say goodbye.*

Whitney's train was leaving before mine. She hugged me hard before walking away, her duffel bag bumping against her thigh. I tried to take a picture of her in my mind. Violet dress, strappy gold sandals, curls as tall as the clouds.

I waited for my train to come at one of the tables by Shake Shack, eating fries out of a paper bag. I let myself think about everything. About the phone call with my mom and with Summer, my conversation with Mrs. Parekh, the ripped jeans that I was too afraid to wear. How people can turn from strangers to secret-keepers. I kept thinking while I crumpled up my greasy bag and headed for tunnel twenty-seven, back under the stars. It was all too much to keep inside. Every once in a while I would have to poke my head out of my shell and sing about it.

Chapter Thirty-Two

The Return

Mom wrapped me up in her arms on the *Bienvenidos* mat. She smelled like cleaning spray and oranges, her after-hospital smell. I squeezed her back and breathed it all in. Edgar came running across the living room, the plush clown-fish in his hand. He gripped my thigh.

Dad stepped in behind me with my duffel bag.

"How was it?" Mom asked into my hair.

"It was wonderful," I said, my cheek against her chest.

"I told her to save all her stories for dinner," Dad said. "We can hear them together."

"Dinner!" Edgar screamed. Dad scooped him up.

"Let Lenny settle in first."

I pulled away from Mom. Everything was the same. Mom's scrubs with the cats in bow ties, Edgar's voice. But my heart felt different. I *did* need to settle into this new world where I didn't hide my Lyric Libro in the closet. A world where Summer and I might not be best friends.

Upstairs my room was too warm, the window sealed up and closing out the breeze. I opened it as far as it could go. Summer's blinds were down. I went to put my duffel bag on my bed and saw an open envelope lying on the comforter. Mom had written *great job* on the outside. The Franklin City Middle School shield was in the corner. I pulled the letter from inside and unfolded it. My classes were listed on one side, the grades on the other. I'd gotten an A in earth science and algebra. An A in art class and history. Ms. Debra had given me an A for gym and wrote *conscientious effort* as a comment. Language Arts was listed last. A-.

I waited for that little minus sign to crush me, but it didn't. It didn't subtract anything from who I was, or who I could be. It was just a little dash. And maybe I'd get more little dashes next year, or in high school, or college. I'd be okay, even if I wasn't always perfect.

Wind came through the window, a relief from the heat. I sat at the end of my bed and faced the *Spread Your Wings* wall. The Post-its were bright between the magazine pages. I could read some of them from here. *It's good to talk about relatable things. OMG those donuts look amazing.*

A pebble flew between me and the wall. It landed on the floor and skidded into the closet.

"Shoot," I heard Summer's voice say. I read one more Post-it. *Do you think it's hard to put your true feelings in an essay?* Summer had written that one.

She was in her window when I got to mine.

"It was open too wide," she said.

"I wasn't expecting you," I answered.

"Yeah." She looked down and dropped a pebble to the grass. "Do you want to take a walk?"

I nodded. Summer disappeared from the window. I ran my fingers over the *write your feelings* Post-it on my way out. Mom called out to me from the kitchen when I got to the front door.

"Hey, dinner's in an hour."

It was so normal, what she'd say every time I rushed out the door to meet Summer. She never even had to ask if that's where I was going.

"I'll be back," I said. Summer was at her mailbox already.

"Summer is welcome to come for dinner too."

My heart thudded. I left before I could answer, or picture Summer in her seat at our dining table. She was opening and closing the mouth of her whale mailbox when I got outside. She had her hair pulled up and sneakers on, but not the ones with my signature.

"Where to?" I asked.

Summer shrugged.

"Let's just walk."

We started up Daybury Street. The sun was hot and made the pavement glow. We turned right at the top of the road.

"Are you happy to be back?" Summer asked. A car zipped by us and we pressed closer to the curb.

"Sort of. I missed home. But now I miss things like the hotel room and swiping my MetroCard. And the Flyers." I imagined Whitney, Cailin, and Harlow walking with us down the street: Whitney wearing something fabulous, Harlow investigating the neighborhood, Cailin taking pictures of the trees.

"I still can't believe you met Magnet," Summer said.

"She prefers Cailin."

Summer turned onto the trail through the woods and I followed. The shade was cool and the trail was hard-packed dirt. Someone had come to clear the overgrown weeds away.

"I missed you," Summer said, then ran ahead and jumped the log in the middle of the path. When she was over, she turned around. She kept her eyes on the wood.

"Me too." I stepped carefully over the log. Summer smiled at the dirt.

The trail opened up to a view of the water, bright blue and glittering. The FRANKLIN CITY BOAT LAUNCH sign was ahead by the stone wall. We both stopped short.

"Is it okay that we came here?" she asked.

"I don't know."

"It's still the same."

"But we're not."

Summer sighed. She rose up on her toes and fell back down, doing nervous calf stretches.

"It's my fault," she said.

My instinct was to tell her she hadn't done anything wrong. But that's not how problems get solved. Diagnoses don't get treated by ignoring them.

"It's mine, too. I didn't speak up when you did things that bothered me. I was too scared of losing you."

The sun on the water was so bright it was hard to look right at it, but I did anyway, let it burn my eyes.

"I'm just as afraid of losing you," Summer said.

"You haven't been acting like that."

"You're my other half, Elena. You have been since we were babies. And I don't want that to be different but lately *I've* been feeling . . . different. I didn't know how to tell you. Or anyone. So I pushed you away instead."

"Tell me what?"

Summer took off.

"Summer!" I called out. I ran after her down the hill toward the boat launch. We stopped at the stone wall.

"I like Riah," she said. She put a hand to the pulse point on her neck.

I wanted to roll my eyes but resisted the urge.

"Yeah, we've established that."

"No." Summer shook her head hard. "I *like* her. Like her."

I thought about Mindy and what she'd said to me in the hall at the Tappiston, about how discovering yourself was like learning a new language. And that friends figured out how to translate. I wrapped my arms around her, breathed in her powdery smell.

"I hear you," I said. "I understand."

Summer squeezed me back.

"Really?" she asked.

"Of course. Did you really think I'd judge you?"

I pulled away. Out on the dock one white boat was being set up by a guy in a cowboy hat, two little kids waiting next to him on the dock in orange lifejackets. The name on the side said *The Jack & Jill*.

"I didn't know what you'd say," she added. "I don't know what anyone's going to say. My parents. Everyone at school."

The man in the cowboy hat stepped into the boat and picked each kid up to bring them on board, then pushed away from the dock.

"Well, I'm here for you. We shouldn't have to hide, especially not from each other," I said.

Summer looked at me, her eyes like sparkling green sea glass.

"Elena, I didn't mean the things you heard me say to Kendra. I've just always known that you could be more than you thought you could. But you didn't see it. You needed more time. And I shouldn't have been upset with you for that."

The *Jack & Jill* sailed farther away, the mechanical sound of its engine getting quieter.

"I see it now." I leaned my shoulder into hers. "So. Does she like you back?"

Summer's smile stretched across her whole face, and she nodded fast. She told me more about Riah, about the butterflies in her stomach when she saw her in the hall, the calmness that overcame her when their steps synched up on a run. The *Jack & Jill* was a speck on the horizon now, and neither of us talked about sailing away, only what was good about being right here.

Chapter
Thirty-Three

The Release Day

Summer and I still inhaled issues of *Spread Your Wings* like we did Bugles. But I looked at them a little differently. Now I knew it was really Gertrude giving the advice in the Ask Amelia section. I knew what the donuts from the Donut Hole tasted like. I knew how it felt to be a Flyer.

The day the September issue was set to release, I was working on a song. My window was open and the fall air slipped through, cool with the smell of leaves.

If you wait until the moment's right
You'll be waiting for the rest of your life.

Footsteps scrambled up the stairs. I looked up in time to see Riah and Summer burst into the room. Their faces were flushed red and sweaty, their sneakers coated in dirt.

My signature was still on Summer's right sneaker, for good luck. Riah's name was on the other.

"Oh my gosh, you are not allowed on this bed," I exclaimed. I starfished myself over the covers.

"We're being punished for working hard?" Summer asked. She pretended she was going to jump on top of me.

"You're glistening!" I laughed.

"What if we have this?" Riah asked. She pulled her hands out from behind her back. A magazine was in one of them, showing the back cover with an ad for fruit-flavored ChapStick. My heart sped up. Summer took my moment of distraction to dive onto the bed, and I was too panicked to think about her sweating on my comforter. Riah handed me the magazine and then grabbed my desk chair, rolling it closer to us. My phone beeped next to me. The screen showed a message from Whitney in the CHEW group chat.

Whitney: VIDEO CHAT TIME?!

Harlow: Yes, I've been staring at this ChapStick ad for so long I'm about to buy the gooseberry flavor.

Cailin: I'm ready!

I opened the laptop I had borrowed from Mom and got the video call app open. It rang a few times, and then Whitney, Harlow, and Cailin appeared on the screen. We had video chatted a few times since we left New York. It was funny to see them in their little boxes, like four worlds coming together. Whitney with her room painted pink, Harlow in front of a big window with a rosebush behind the glass, Cailin with her cheerleading bows and trophies on the wall.

"Summer and Riah are here too," I said, and flipped the computer so they could see.

"Hey," Cailin replied, and Summer's mouth dropped open. This was the third time they'd virtually met, but Summer still got tongue-tied around Cailin, which was funny since that used to be me. Well, words still got tangled in my head. But I was better about getting them out. We had eighth-grade orientation a week ago, and when the guidance counselor, Mr. Douglas, asked if anyone did anything fun this summer, I raised my hand and talked about being a Flyer, and only blushed a little bit.

A tall teenage boy swooped into the screen behind Harlow. He ruffled Harlow's hair before disappearing out of the shot.

"Hey!" she squealed, covering her head with her hands. Denny flew back across the room with a book. He went for her hair again but Harlow was ready this time. She was grinning when she turned to the camera again.

"I'm glad you and your brother made up," Cailin said.

Harlow looked in the direction Denny had gone. Light poured in through the window behind her.

"Me too. I realized I just had to turn it into an interview. Ask him all the questions I wanted to know about why he did what he did. And he told me the truth."

"What was it?" Whitney asked.

Harlow's face settled into what I now recognized as her reporter face.

"Sorry. That's classified."

"So he's not a stupid dumb stupidface anymore?" I asked. Summer and Riah giggled into their hands on either side of me.

"He for sure still is. But only in the normal brother way now."

Whitney cleared her throat.

"Not to interrupt," she said, bouncing in her chair. "But are we going to look at this magazine we're in?"

We all nodded back. My palms started to sweat.

"On the count of three we flip it over," Harlow said. "One."

"Two," Cailin added.

"Three," Summer, Riah, and I said together, then flipped the magazine to the cover.

The four of us had our heads close, Cailin and me below Whitney and Harlow. It was a shot from Lot 88, and the four of us were smiling so big. The cover was light pink, the *Spread Your Wings* logo above our heads, the contents of the magazine printed around us. *10 Perfect Back to School Outfits. How to Handle a Bully. Ask Amelia: Friend Dilemmas!*

"I love it," Cailin said softly. I ran my hand over the cover and tried to remember every detail of this moment, my friends all around me.

We all started to flip through together, and once in a while someone would ask, "Are you done?" and someone would say, "Almost," and Summer and I looked at each other and knew that our *Spread Your Wings* tradition was only more special now that we were sharing it with Riah and the Flyers. I looked over the outfits Whitney had helped put together, the pictures at the Donut Hole that Cailin had taken, the bullying article Harlow had contributed to. And the Ask Amelia advice that I'd given to Friendless.

Our essay was at the end.

"Should I read it out loud?" I asked.

The Flyers nodded. Summer and Riah came closer.

"We know that this is usually the place where each Flyer writes an essay on what is important to them. But we wanted to do things a little differently, because we went through this week together and thought it was only right to do this part together too. We all showed up to the city with our own baggage. Whether we meant to or not, we carried those heavy items with us here. We packed each other into it when we shouldn't have. Maybe you'll be able to tell that from the pictures, but most likely, you won't.

"We learned that we are capable of more than we thought. We can lift each other up, call each other out, follow our dreams, and, most importantly, tell the truth. To other people, and to ourselves.

"Fly High,

"Cailin, Harlow, Elena, and Whitney

"Your September Flyers."

Summer leaned into my shoulder. I looked at the video chat, at the three other Flyers in squares shaped like the Post-its stuck to my wall. I wasn't sure what the sticky notes might say tomorrow or next week or next year, because life didn't have a table of contents like a magazine.

But I wasn't scared. I had Summer, and the Flyers, and we'd help each other soar no matter what.

AUTHOR'S NOTE

I had a panic attack for the first time in a Price Rite supermarket. I remember thinking my lungs had forgotten how to breathe, that my brain was shutting down its systems. Yet, nothing was wrong. It was a slow weekend morning. It was a produce section. Still, I was convinced I was in immense danger, and the feeling didn't pass until I was back in the car, blasting cold air and taking deep breaths. Like Whitney, I felt like a very small piece of a very big world. A world that felt like it was abruptly ending.

But the world kept turning, as it usually does, no matter how hard your brain tries to tell you it won't. Nothing has to be wrong for anxiety and panic to, well, *attack*. It's an ambush, an enemy swooping in at unexpected times. Often it can feel like you're fighting the battle alone. But like Whitney learns, sharing the load with others can help. Using available resources can help. Finding your own way to get through it can help.

You are going to be okay. And you are not alone.

• • •

Here are a few online resources I've found helpful:

positivepsychology.com/mindfulness-for-children-kids
-activities

childmind.org/topics/concerns/anxiety

adaa.org/living-with-anxiety/children/anxiety-and
-depression

Mobile apps like Calm and Headspace also encourage mindfulness and can help relieve anxiety. Sites like adaa.org can connect those struggling with anxiety and panic to licensed therapists.